THE STUPIDS

Novelization by Clay Griffith

Based on the Screenplay by Brent Forrester

Based on characters created by

Harry Allard and James Marshall

A SKYLARK BOOK

NEW YORK   TORONTO   LONDON   SYDNEY   AUCKLAND

RL 4.6, All Ages

THE STUPIDS

A Skylark Book / February 1996

Skylark Books is a registered trademark of Bantam Books, a division of Bantam Doubleday Dell Publishing Group, Inc. Registered in U.S. Patent and Trademark Office and elsewhere.

ISBN 0-553-48498-2

Published simultaneously in the United States and Canada

Bantam Books are published by Bantam Books, a division of Bantam Doubleday Dell Publishing Group, Inc. Its trademark, consisting of the words "Bantam Books" and the portrayal of a rooster, is Registered in U.S. Patent and Trademark Office and in other countries. Marca Registrada. Bantam Books, 1540 Broadway, New York, New York 10036.

SAVOY PICTURES PRESENTS AN IMAGINE ENTERTAINMENT PRODUCTION A LANDIS/BELZBERG FILM
TOM ARNOLD "THE STUPIDS" JESSICA LUNDY BUG HALL ALEX McKENNA MARK METCALF MATT KEESLAR AND CHRISTOPHER LEE
DEBORAH NADOOLMAN PHIL DAGORT MANFRED GUTHE C.S.C. LESLIE BELZBERG JAMES MARSHALL AND HARRY ALLARD
BRENT FORRESTER BRIAN GRAZER JOHN LANDIS

CREDITS NOT CONTRACTUAL

PRINTED IN THE UNITED STATES OF AMERICA

OPM   0 9 8 7 6 5 4 3 2 1

THE STUPIDS

CONTENTS

A Mystery Full of Garbage

Bang!

When the Universe was created a long time ago, swirling gases became stars and planets. The earth appeared in space! Little cells wriggled in the muck. Then there were fish. And lizards. And dinosaurs. Then mammals. Humans showed up. They used tools and language and built pyramids, temples, castles, and cities. They painted. They wrote poetry. They fought wars. They progressed through the Roman Empire, the Dark Ages, the Renaissance, the Industrial Revolution, and World War II. They split the atom, unleashing the powers of the creation of the Universe! Then came . . . The Stupids.

In a nice house in the suburbs, day was dawning for the Stupids. Sunlight filled the bedroom. Stanley and

Joan Stupid woke up with their feet resting on their pillows and their heads at the foot of the bed. They sat up.

"I've got a feeling something special is going to happen today," said Joan.

Stanley smiled. "My dear, every day I spend with you is special." He got out of bed. He was wearing his pajama tops and boxer shorts and a pair of brown dress shoes.

"Oh, Stanley," Joan said lovingly.

"I love this family, Joan," Stanley proclaimed. "And because of that I'm happy. If that makes me a simple man, well, a simple man I must be. But enough of my speeches. Let's start the day!"

Stanley lit a match and held it up to the sprinkler in the ceiling. Water sprayed everywhere, and Stanley began to scrub himself.

Joan was getting dressed. She put on one sock. Then she looked at her other sock. "Inside out," she observed.

She stuck her hand in the sock, pushing it right side out. But now the sock was on her hand. If she pulled it off, it would be inside out again. Joan took a pair of scissors and cut off the toe of the sock. She yanked the body of the sock all the way up her arm. Then she stretched it over her head. She pulled it down over both shoulders and then past her waist. Then she removed one leg from the sock and pulled the sock down to her bare foot. "Hmm, mmm, hmm," she hummed happily, getting out a needle and thread to sew the end of the sock shut.

In the bathroom, Stanley lathered his face with shaving cream. Then he started to shave with an electric razor. Foam flew everywhere.

Joan went to the kitchen and mixed a big bowl of pancake batter. She handed the bowl to Petunia Stupid, their delightful nine-year-old daughter. Petunia poured the batter into the toaster. Joan called out, "Two fresh waffles, coming up!"

Stanley sat at the kitchen table dressed for work in a suit and sneakers. He read the newspaper. It was still rolled up.

Petunia asked, "What's in the news, Dad?"

Stanley said, "Oh, turmoil in the Middle E—. The president vetoes another b—. A lot of stuff you wouldn't understand."

Buster Stupid, their eight-year-old son, walked into the kitchen. He looked sad. "Hi, Dad. Hi, Mom. Hi, Petunia." He tossed a biscuit to the family dog. "Hi, Kitty."

Stanley said, "Morning, Buster. Say, why the long face?"

"Aw, it's nothing really, Dad," Buster answered. "Just that, well . . . I seem to be shrinking."

Stanley looked at his son. "Shrinking? Are you sure?"

"Positive. Every month I measure myself, and every month the marks get lower." He pointed to a potted tree in the kitchen that had several marks on its trunk. As Petunia watered the tree, Buster said, "When we first got this tree, I was way up here on it, and now I'm way down here. By the time I'm a teenager, I'll barely be up to my own waist!"

Stanley put his arm around Buster's shoulders in a fatherly way. "I know that growing up can be hard, Buster, especially when you're shrinking. But trust in yourself and you'll get through it. Just like I did."

Buster asked, "You mean . . . you were once shrinking too?"

"That's right, son. It was around the time we switched over to the metric system, and I went from over six feet to barely two meters overnight. But I never gave up on myself and somehow I came back. Just like you will."

"Thanks, Dad. I feel better already!"

"That's the spirit, Buster!" Stanley patted his son on the back. "Well, I'm off to work!"

Petunia called, "Have a wonderful day, Dad!"

Joan watched her husband leave. "Marrying that man was the smartest thing I ever did." She sighed happily and continued to iron the bacon.

Stanley paused on the front porch and pulled out a list. "Things to do today. *Make check mark on paper.*" He made a check mark on the paper. "*Cross item out.*" He crossed the next item out. "No time for that, I'm afraid. *Scratch head.*" He scratched his head. "Hmm . . . I'll have to think about that one. *Hum to myself.* Hmm, mmm. And finally, say *That seems*

4

pretty senseless but whatever. Huh. That seems pretty senseless." He shrugged. "But whatever."

Stanley walked to the curb and saw two trash cans sitting there. "That's odd." He yelled back to the house. "Joan, honey! Did you put these trash cans out on the curb?"

Joan came out of the house. "Of course, Stanley. Everyone in the neighborhood displays their trash cans on Thursdays. It's garbage can celebration day."

Stanley said, "But today is Friday."

Joan gasped. "I left the trash cans out overnight!"

Stanley lifted the lid from one of the garbage cans and looked inside. Then he gasped. "Oh dear!" He peered into the second trash can. "Oh no!" He looked at Joan. "Somebody's stolen our garbage again!"

Later, Stanley and Joan were in their kitchen discussing the garbage crisis. Joan dipped a tea bag into a cup of hot water. Stanley dunked a bag of coffee into a pot of hot water.

Joan said, "I just feel so awful about this."

"Darling, please, it's not your fault," Stanley said. "It's the world we live in today! There are people out there for whom nothing is sacred anymore. People who steal a man's garbage, week after week after week!"

Joan sipped her tea. "We can get through it, honey," she said. "We'll borrow some garbage until we get back on our feet."

Stanley argued, "But don't you see, Joan? That's

what they're counting on. Whoever keeps doing this knows that people like us will just sit back and take it." He stood up dramatically. "Well, darn it! I'm not going to take it anymore!"

"Stanley, please. Don't get involved!" Joan begged.

"I'm already involved, Joan! Someone has stolen from my family. And I won't rest until I bring them to justice!" Stanley marched into the garage to plan. Joan watched him go. She just adored him.

That night, Stanley's scheme was coming together. He dropped items into a trash can. "Two banana peels. One bicycle rim, bent. Section C of the Sunday *Times*. Three alkaline batteries. One grapefruit rind . . ." He gazed proudly at his trap. "Just try to resist this, you fiends."

Stanley dragged the trash can outside and put it by the curb. He hid behind a nearby bush and watched the garbage. Every time a car passed by, he would perk up. Then a man with a dog stopped next to the trash can. Stanley stared at him. This would be it! The garbage thief! Then the man moved on. Stanley continued to wait. Eventually he fell asleep. And he slept through the night.

An early-morning loud noise woke him up. Stanley sat up as a large truck rumbled to a stop at the curb. There was a strange bluish light. Two men, wearing gloves and masks, got out of the truck and approached the trash can.

"What in the world . . . ," Stanley wondered as he watched the two men. They grabbed the garbage can and emptied it into the back of the truck. They got back into the truck and it started off down the street.

Stanley leapt from the bush. "They're getting away!" He raced into the garage. "I've got to follow them! But how?" He looked frantically around the garage. He saw a bicycle. "Two wheels." Then he saw the station wagon. "Four wheels." Then he saw a pair of in-line skates. "Eight wheels!"

As the garbage truck rolled through the streets of town, Stanley raced after it on skates. "All right, crooks! Now you've got Stanley Stupid on your trail."

In the Stupids' kitchen, Petunia Stupid was eating breakfast. Her brother, Buster, entered the kitchen.

"Morning, Buster," she said.

"Hey, Sis. Have you seen Dad?"

Petunia said, "Isn't he sleeping?"

"No," Buster answered. "And he's not outside either." Buster was pulling a wagon with a goldfish bowl in it. "I got up early to walk my fish and he was already gone."

Petunia stared at Buster. "Do you think maybe . . . he's been kidnapped?"

"Oh my God!" Buster shouted. "We must go to the police station!"

Petunia handed Buster a pad of paper and a pencil. "Just as soon as we've left a note for Mom. Take this down! We have gone to the police."

Buster struggled to write down what Petunia was saying. *"Police . . ."*

"Dad has been kidnapped."

". . . kidnapped . . . ," Buster repeated.

Petunia continued to dictate. "Don't worry, we'll be back soon. Signed, *Your Children.*"

". . . your children," Buster scrawled.

Petunia grabbed Buster. "Let's move!" They raced out the door.

The family cat jumped up on the table and looked at the note left behind—*"Police Kidnapped Your Children."* The cat sighed and shook her head.

Later that morning, Joan Stupid was looking around the house for her family. She looked into the bedroom. "Stanley?" She poked her head into the kitchen. "Buster? Petunia?" She came into the kitchen. "Stanley? Buster? Petunia? Where is everybody?"

She found the note on the table and read it. She exclaimed, "No. It's impossible! It can't be true!"

The phone rang. "Hello?" she answered.

On the other end of the phone was a police officer. He was sitting at the station with Petunia and Buster beside him. "Hello," he said. "Is this Mrs. Stupid?"

"Yes . . ."

"I'm calling from the police station, Mrs. Stupid. We have your children here, ma'am."

"Oh my God, it is true!" Joan slammed the phone down. "The police have kidnapped my children!"

She put on her coat and grabbed her car keys. She yanked open a door and ran right into the closet. *Oops!* The door opened and Joan popped out, charging out of the house to save her children.

Stanley was still chasing the garbage truck downtown. He skated over cars that were stuck in line because of a traffic jam. He went up and down over trunks and roofs. Then down and up again over hoods and roofs. Suddenly—*whoops!*—he dropped through a car's sunroof. He left via the passenger door and climbed onto the rear of the next car. Then he continued the chase—up and down, up and down. Motorists stared, unable to believe what they were seeing.

Nearby, a police officer was driving Petunia and Buster back home. The police officer looked into the backseat, where the kids sat. "You two just sit tight," he said. "We'll have you home in a minute."

None of the others saw Joan Stupid speeding past them in the opposite direction. She was thinking furiously of ways to free her children from the police.

The garbage truck stopped at a red light. Stanley rolled up on the sidewalk next to it. The driver of the truck glanced out at Stanley.

The driver was looking at him: Stanley tried to

blend in. He crossed his arms and casually leaned against a lamppost. His feet slipped and slid, skittering wildly in the in-line skates. Stanley grabbed on to the lamppost to hold himself up. He still tried to look casual. The driver stared at him. Stanley hummed and inspected his fingernails. Finally he joined several little girls nearby in a game of hopscotch.

The traffic light turned green and the truck roared off. Stanley waited for a moment, whistling to himself, pretending not to notice the truck. Then he took off after it.

Back at the Stupids' house, Petunia and Buster searched for their mother. "Mom? Mom?" They checked closets and looked under the couch cushions.

Petunia said, "It's no use, Buster. Mom's gone too."

Buster exclaimed, "And we seem to be caught in a deadly game of cat and mouse!"

"Buster, look!" Petunia pointed out the window.

Outside, an Asian man stepped to their front door for a second, then turned and walked away. The children rushed out the front door and looked up the street in both directions.

Petunia said, "He left without even ringing the bell."

"Apparently he only wanted us to find *this*!" Buster held up a take-out menu from a Chinese restaurant that had been left near the front door.

Petunia studied the menu. "What's The Jade Palace? And what does it have to do with Dad and Mom?"

"I don't know, Petunia. But I think it's time we went there and found out. Come on!"

The kids jumped on their bikes and pedaled away.

Joan was driving down the street, looking around for signs of her family. She spoke into what she thought was a microcassette recorder. "Saturday, June fourth. Today my world turned upside down. First I discovered my husband missing. Then I learned that the police had kidnapped my children. Now the fate of my family rests in my hands. Note to myself: I must buy a handheld tape recorder. Then I will no longer be speaking into a garage door opener." She clicked the garage door opener.

Nearby, a garage door began to open. It hit the bottom of a ladder that was set up in front of it. The man on the ladder toppled over. The can of white paint he was using to paint the garage door went flying. Across the street, a pair of gang members were spray-painting the wall. The can of paint splattered over their graffiti, whitewashing the wall completely clean.

"Aw, man!" one gang member said.

The other member complained, "Some people are so thoughtless."

Petunia and Buster scraped to a stop in front of The Jade Palace Chinese restaurant. They entered and stared at the porcelain vases and fans and silk clothes with dragons and tigers on them.

A young Chinese woman walked up to them, smiled, and said, "Just the two of you?"

Buster was shocked. "Why . . . yes."

"So they *have* been expecting us," Petunia whispered to her brother.

Back on the streets, Stanley was exhausted from chasing the garbage truck. When it stopped at another red light, he caught up with it. He was gasping for breath. "Must . . . rest . . ." He lay down on the platform on the back of the truck. He quickly fell asleep, and the truck drove on, with Stanley snoozing in the back.

In The Jade Palace, Petunia and Buster were sitting at a table. They glanced around suspiciously. A waiter approached them.

"And what can I get for you?" the waiter asked.

Petunia eyed him slyly. "Oh, I think you've got a pretty good idea what we're looking for."

The waiter said, "May I recommend the cashew chicken?"

Petunia snapped back, "You'll get your cash when we get our parents back."

"And don't call us chicken," Buster growled.

The garbage truck pulled into a truck stop on the highway. The driver got out to buy a cup of coffee.

Stanley suddenly woke up. He bolted to his feet, staring at the large, empty parking lot.

"Oh my gosh!" he shouted. "The truck! It's gone! I've lost it. And now it could be anywhere!" He looked to the left and right, but not behind him, where the large truck sat. "Catching up with it now will be like finding a needle in a haystack!"

The driver got back into the truck and started it. As the truck began to drive off, Stanley whirled around. His eyes lit up.

"It's always in the last place you'd think of looking," Stanley said. And off he skated, after the garbage truck again.

Stanley Gets His Name in the Paper

Petunia and Buster ate Chinese food. Buster was trying to eat with chopsticks that were still in the paper wrapper. "I'll never get the hang of these things," he complained.

Petunia took a mushu pancake and wiped her face with it. She crumpled it up like a napkin and threw it away. "Still no sign of Mom and Dad. I don't get it, Buster."

"Don't worry," Buster said. "Whoever brought us here will contact us when the time is right."

The waiter cleared their plates and set down two fortune cookies. Buster grabbed one and stuffed it into his mouth. Petunia looked at her brother chewing the cookie and saw something strange. "Buster! It's a message!"

She pulled the little strip of paper out of his

14

mouth. She read it. *"Time flies when you're having fun."*

Buster said, "Time flies when you're having fun? Wait a minute. Isn't the *Daily Times* published just a few blocks from here?"

"Yes," Petunia said, "at the corner of Fun Street and Fly!"

"No, it's Maple and Fifth."

"Close enough," Petunia retorted. "Let's move!"

The garbage truck arrived at the landfill. It was a huge open area full of giant piles of garbage. The truck dumped its garbage into one of the piles.

Nearby, Stanley was hiding and watching. He was disguised. He had one bush tied to his back and another one tied to his chest. "Camouflage, lesson one," Stanley said to himself. "To look like a bush, you must *think* like a bush." He paused and concentrated, straining to think like a bush. "Well, here I am, being a bush. Just growing and hanging out, that's the life for me."

He began to crawl slowly toward the garbage collectors. "Sure is a lot of soil around here. Lots of sunshine too. As a bush, I notice these things, yes sir. But wait, what's this?" He held out his arms and looked at them. "I have arms. I'm a bush with arms. And legs!" He stood up. "I'm the first bush in history with legs! I—*can*—*walk*!" He took a few stiff steps.

"Gaze ye, unbelievers," he exclaimed, "upon this miracle, this walking bush! Half plant, half man, he

15

dwells in two worlds, master of both! Oh, man-bush! You are nature's greatest wonder!"

The garbage collectors climbed back into their truck. They glanced at Stanley for a second. He froze. The garbage collectors shook their heads and drove off.

Stanley snickered. "The poor fools thought I was a bush."

Petunia and Buster rode to the *Daily Times* building on their bikes. "This is the place," Buster announced.

Petunia said grimly, "Let's do it."

She pulled out a bike lock. She and Buster chained their bikes to a pole at the curb. They walked to the door of the building. They didn't notice that the pole to which they chained their bikes was the door handle of a bus. The bus roared off down the road, dragging their bikes along with it.

At that same moment, Joan Stupid drove by and saw Petunia and Buster on the sidewalk. "My children!" She slammed on the brakes. Behind her, cars screeched wildly and slammed into each other.

She jumped out of the station wagon. But she saw a uniformed crossing guard on the sidewalk near the *Daily Times* building. She stopped. "Police! If they recognize me, I'm sure to be kidnapped too. What to do?"

She searched the street and saw the sign WIG STORE. She raced into the store and ran up to the counter, where a clerk stood. "I need a wig, please." She glanced back out the window at the crossing guard. "In fact, I'm going to need a lot of wigs."

Back at the landfill, Stanley was beginning to realize how big the place was. He stared through the foliage of the bush that was attached to him. "My gosh. There must be thousands of people's garbage here. Tens of thousands, even. Why, the sheer organization necessary to pull off a heist like this . . ." He thought about it. "I've uncovered the crime of the century."

Joan strolled innocently down the sidewalk. She had wigs pinned to every inch of her clothing. Passing by the crossing guard, she tried not to appear suspicious. Her breathing was shallow and she began to perspire. "Good day, Officer," she said with a smile.

She scurried past him and slipped into the *Daily Times* building. She leaned back against the wall and clenched her fist in triumph. "Yes!"

A large black limousine sped down the dirt road that ran to the far end of the landfill. It screeched to a stop. A burly man jumped out and opened the back door. A foreign-looking man in a uniform stepped out of the back of the limousine. He and the driver walked past a line of other black limousines. Then they joined a group of military men, some wearing uniforms of many different countries, some dressed in very expensive suits. They all wore dark sunglasses.

Nearby, a colonel in the U.S. Army leaned on the hood of a Jeep, watching the crowd gather. He turned to the lieutenant who stood next to him.

"Is that everyone?" the colonel asked.

"Affirmative, sir. It's show time."

The colonel stood up and addressed the group. "Welcome, gentlemen. I hope you'll forgive the unpleasantness of our surroundings. This setting was chosen for its seclusion, not its beauty." He threw back a tarpaulin that covered the back of the Jeep. Under it were a variety of sophisticated military weapons. "The weapons you are about to see are American made and, I humbly submit, the world's best. International law has long kept you from acquiring them. But as of now, I hope to help you overcome that. Lieutenant?"

The lieutenant stepped forward with two American soldiers. He announced, "The first piece of equipment we'd like to demonstrate is the Dragon antitank missile. Whether you want to foment revolution or suppress it, this hardware will help you get it done."

Stanley, still disguised as a bush, wandered into the back of the crowd of foreign soldiers and politicians.

Stanley was musing. "Strange indeed are the workings of fate. How could I have known that today I would wander into the jaws of some kind of supercrime?" He stepped around a man wearing a turban. "Excuse me," he said aloud. Then he continued

18

thinking. "Chances are, my life is already in danger. Yet I feel strangely, intensely alive. Every nerve is alert, every sense working overtime. Nothing escapes my eye."

He bumped into a Latin American revolutionary who was leaning on an AK-47 assault rifle. "Pardon me." He stopped for a minute as some of the world's most dangerous men stared at him. He didn't notice them. He was thinking, "One journey has come to an end. But I've got a feeling the real adventure has just begun."

Wearing her multiwig dress, Joan wandered through the halls of the *Daily Times* building. Then she saw Petunia and Buster coming toward her. She called out, "Buster! Petunia!"

The children screamed.

"It's some kind of ape woman!" Petunia shouted.

"No," Joan said to her, "it's me, your mother!"

Buster turned to Petunia in shock. "Your mother's some kind of ape woman?"

Joan said, "No, children. It's a disguise."

The kids' looks went from horror to admiration. They both went, "Ahhhhh . . ."

At the landfill, the lieutenant pulled a tarp off a fancy missile launcher. "And now the cream of the crop. The eighty-millimeter M224 with computer visual targeting system, known in the media as the Smart Bomb. And how smart it is."

He set the viewfinder on an old junked car in the distance. The computer read LOCK ON—TARGET. He fired the missile. The viewfinder stayed locked on the old car as the missile flew swiftly across the landfill, dead on target. The missile hit and the car exploded.

Stanley didn't notice the explosion. He wandered through the crowd. He was taking notes on a little pad, but then his pen ran out of ink. He turned to a huge bodyguard standing next to him.

"Excuse me." Stanley held up his old pen. "You have something I can write with?"

The bodyguard stared at Stanley. Then he opened his coat to reveal a shoulder holster with a huge pistol. He reached into his pocket and pulled out a pen for Stanley.

"Thanks," Stanley said. "So . . . what's going on here, some kind of company picnic?"

The bodyguard said, *"Farouzh bharghati."*

Stanley nodded. "That's a very festive name for it." He lowered his voice and leaned over to the bodyguard. "Listen, you might as well hear it here first. You notice all the garbage around here? All stolen. Something fishy's going on here. Frankly, our lives may be in danger."

The bodyguard said, *"Bhagavasha khozeni."*

"Yeah, I hear you, pal," Stanley agreed. "At first I was pretty tongue-tied myself."

Back at the *Daily Times*, two reporters were laboring at a computer, working up a headline for the newspaper. On the computer screen was the headline— "Cult Leader Picks University Site." There was a picture next to it of the white-haired Reverend Wright.

One reporter said, "Man, I'd be scared to have my name on an article like that. This guy Reverend Wright is dangerous."

"Oh, relax," the second reporter responded. "Wright's just another phony preacher who steals from his flock."

"That's what they said about Jim Jones, my friend."

"If you ask me, Wright's a con man, nothing more."

Suddenly their editor rushed up. "What are you two standing around for? I got stories breaking on the AP wire!"

"Just working on this headline, sir."

The editor read the screen. "Cult Leader Picks University Site." He hit a key, a little red light flashed, and the computer began to grind. "Your work is done. Now, let's move!" The three men hurried off together.

Buster peeked around the corner of the office. "Psst, over here, Sis. I found a computer!"

Petunia crept in after him, pulling her mother behind her.

"What do you have in mind?" Joan asked.

Petunia sat down at the computer the three men had just left. "A little ride on the information superhighway, Mom. In this age of microtechnology, the computer is our gateway to information. All we've got to do is figure out the password."

The three Stupids thought hard. Buster scratched his nose, as he often did when he was thinking. Then he had an inspiration.

He said, "How about . . . NOSE?"

Petunia said, "It's worth a try!"

She typed in the word NOSE. She didn't notice that she was changing the layout of the headline on the screen. She hit a key. A little red light flashed and the computer began to grind.

Petunia exclaimed, "Something's happening!"

Joan praised them. "Way to go, kids!"

"All right, computer," Petunia said. "Now tell us everything we need to know about . . ." She typed, "STANLEYSTUPID."

The computer screen changed the headline again. Now it read "Cult Leader Picks Nose." And the author of the story was now Stanley Stupid.

A short time later, the *Daily Times* was delivered. In the offices of the Reverend Wright's ministry, the reverend sat in his plush office studying his budget. A painting of the soon-to-be-built Reverend Wright University hung on the wall behind him. His assistant stood next to him.

The Reverend Wright asked, "How much am I claiming the university will cost?"

"Eighty million dollars, sir," the assistant answered.

The Reverend Wright smiled and said, "Make it ninety. I want to buy a Learjet." He laughed.

The assistant looked upset, but he just said, "If you insist, Reverend."

The reverend stared at his assistant angrily. "Do you question my judgment?"

"No sir." The assistant shook his head quickly. "It's just that . . . I'd hate for people to say that you were dishonest."

The Reverend Wright's face turned bright red. He was fuming. "Have you forgotten that there is a *war* going on in this country? I am a soldier, chosen by the Almighty to fight heathen forces spearheaded by a conspiracy in the liberal media to hack away at our nation's moral foundation! And now you want to question that."

The assistant said meekly, "I'm sorry, sir."

One of the reverend's followers entered the room with a tray of coffee and the latest edition of the daily paper. He was wearing a satin jacket embroidered with the face of the Reverend Wright on the back along with the words "If It Isn't Wright, It's Wrong."

As he picked up the newspaper, the Reverend Wright snarled at his assistant. "You'd better be sorry. The reverend knows more of wrath than he does of mercy." He looked at the headline of the paper—"Cult Leader Picks Nose."

His face turned even darker red. His eyes narrowed into hateful slits. He read the name of the author and shouted, "Find me this man, Stanley Stupid!"

The colonel and the lieutenant watched from a distance as some of their men continued demonstrating the weapons to the international terrorists and madmen. The lieutenant looked nervous. He wiped his face with a handkerchief.

The colonel smiled confidently. "Relax, soldier. A week from now we'll both be wealthy men."

The lieutenant took a sharp breath. "I suppose so, sir. But I can't help wondering what our country would think of what we're doing."

The colonel stopped smiling. "This year, our country refused my promotion, Lieutenant. They have only themselves to blame."

"Y-You really think we can pull this off?" The lieutenant stammered.

The colonel lit a cigar and took a puff. "I gave my life to the military. And nothing's going to stop me from getting something back."

Suddenly a very nervous soldier rushed up to the colonel and saluted. "Sir, I think we may have a potential situation on our hands!"

"What is it, soldier?" the colonel asked calmly.

"An individual, sir, appears to have infiltrated the proceedings. As far as we can tell, he's not affiliated with the buyers."

The lieutenant shouted, "Holy cow! It's the CIA. We're probably already surrounded!"

"Negative," the soldier said. "We've scouted the area and he appears to be alone."

"Alone?" the lieutenant asked.

The colonel said, "Just what kind of cowboy agent is this guy?" He pulled out his binoculars and scanned the area. He saw Stanley in the distance, examining a rubber inner tube. Stanley stretched the inner tube, then got tangled up in it.

The colonel turned to the soldier and barked, "No one is to disturb him without my order. The buyers mustn't know anything is amiss."

"Understood, sir." The soldier marched off.

The colonel said, "If I know my business, the operative will contact us."

The lieutenant took the binoculars and stared at Stanley. "To walk into a situation like this, without support . . . This guy must be fearless."

Stanley hooked one foot in the inner tube and stretched it out as far as it would go. Then it snapped back and knocked him off his feet.

"Yes," the colonel agreed. "And very, very smart."

At the *Daily Times* office, Petunia, Buster, and Joan were still crowded in front of the computer. A copy of the newspaper scrolled past them on the screen.

Joan said, "Business, weather, sports. What is it trying to tell us?"

Petunia said, "It's computer jargon, Mom. It's like

a whole other language. Now, hand me a photo of Dad and let's see what we can find out."

Joan took a picture of Stanley out of her wallet and handed it to her daughter. Petunia slid the photo into the computer's disk drive. The computer began to make loud grinding noises. Smoke poured out of the back.

Petunia said confidently, "It's processing data."

The computer beeped and printed something on the screen.

"What does it say?" Joan asked.

Petunia read the screen, "Fatal error, drive B."

"Oh my Lord!" Joan shouted.

Buster asked, "What does it mean?"

Petunia yelled, "I don't *know*!"

Joan was near hysteria. "We've got to warn your father!"

Across the newsroom, all the computers were sparking and smoking. People shouted and ran around. No one knew what was happening.

Buster said, "We'd better get out of here."

"Let's go!" Petunia called out.

The three Stupids rushed out of the *Daily Times* building. The kids looked around. They didn't see their bikes. They didn't even see the pole they had chained their bikes to.

Buster shouted, "The bikes are gone!"

Joan saw that a meter maid was placing a parking ticket on her station wagon. The car was sitting in the middle of the street.

She exclaimed, "And the cops have surrounded my car!"

Petunia shouted, "Run for your lives!"

The three Stupids raced away down the sidewalk.

Stanley Stupid— the Human Target 3

Stanley stood in a long line of foreign soldiers and revolutionaries. They were passing by the colonel and shaking his hand as they left the demonstration. The colonel greeted them all, speaking a few words. "Until we meet again . . . *Adiós* . . . *Au revoir* . . . *Allahu akhbar* . . . *Danke schön* . . ."

Then Stanley shook the colonel's hand. "Hi. Stanley Stupid."

The colonel stared at him coldly. "Honored to make your acquaintance, Mr. Stupid. You must be quite a skilled investigator to have discovered all this."

Stanley smiled a little. "Well, I knew I was on the trail of some crafty thieves. But I didn't realize I'd find this much garbage."

One soldier got angry. He thought Stanley was

talking about him, and he reached for his gun. The colonel raised his hand and calmed the soldier.

The colonel said to Stanley, "You're clearly an agent of enormous talents. It's a shame the government will never reward you as richly as you deserve."

Stanley shrugged. "No, I doubt the government even knows I'm here."

"And that's why you've approached me, isn't it?" the colonel asked. "To come and get your share, one way or another."

Stanley shook his head. "Well, mister, to tell the truth, I approached you because I need a car."

The colonel said quickly, "Lieutenant, give our friend the keys to my car." He smiled at Stanley. "A gift to the gifted."

Stanley took the keys from the lieutenant. He couldn't believe his good luck. "Wow! That's really generous of you." He got into the big government sedan. "And to think I really only wanted a ride back to town." He waved at the crowd of the world's most dangerous men. "Thanks, everybody!" Then Stanley drove away.

The lieutenant watched the car disappear through the landfill. He said, "So blackmail's his game."

The colonel agreed. "Just as I thought."

The lieutenant shook his head in amazement. "Talk about nerves of steel. Completely surrounded and he didn't even blink."

The soldier standing nearby said, "So we bought

him off for now, sir. But what's to stop him from turning us in anyway?''

"You are, soldier." The colonel gazed at the soldier. He cocked a gun and handed it to the young man. "Wait until all our clients have long since departed. Then terminate the target with extreme prejudice.''

"Yes *sir*." The soldier started to leave. Then he turned back, looking confused. "Meaning?"

"Kill him.''

"Right!" The soldier trotted away.

Joan, Petunia, and Buster burst into their house. They quickly locked the door behind them. They stood there trying to catch their breath.

Joan exclaimed, "You never realize how many police officers there are until the day they turn against you.''

Buster held his head. He was afraid. "What kind of madness have we gotten into? It's the biggest emergency of our lives and we can't even call 9-1-1!''

Petunia said, "You're right, Buster. A crisis like this calls for an even higher authority." She turned to Joan. "Mom, dial 10-1-1!"

Joan thought for a second. "I'm afraid that's not good enough, children. Your father's life is on the line." She grabbed the phone with great determination. "And I'm calling 100,470,355,011!" She began to push buttons on the phone with incredible speed.

In a few seconds, a phone rang in a surf shop in

Australia. The owner, wearing khaki shorts and a bush hat and holding a huge can of beer, answered the phone. "G'day, mate."

Joan Stupid answered, "Hello. My name is Joan Stupid. My husband, Stanley, is missing and I need you to help me find him!"

The Australian laughed. "Gee, ma'am, we mostly just sell surfboards here. But if your husband comes into the shop, we'll tell him to phone home."

"Bless you," Joan said. She hung up the phone. "We can relax now, kids. The most sophisticated emergency response team in the world is working with us." She paused, then said, "Interestingly, they mostly just sell surfboards there."

The phone rang and she picked it up. "Hello?"

"Hi, honey, it's me!" Stanley said. He was talking on a cellular phone in the colonel's car.

"Stanley!" Joan shouted with joy. "Darling, are you all right?"

"I'm fine," Stanley assured her. "But you won't believe the things I've uncovered."

Joan whispered into the phone in case the line was tapped. "Stanley, listen to me closely. You must beware of the drive bee!"

"What's the drive bee?" Stanley asked.

"We don't know," Joan replied. "But any error you make with it could be fatal!"

Stanley nodded knowingly. "Just as I suspected. My life may already be in jeopardy."

Stanley didn't notice the Jeep following his car.

The soldier who had been instructed to kill Stanley leaned out of the passenger's side of the Jeep. He had a pistol in his hand. He fired at Stanley, but he hit the gas tank of the car instead. Gas began to spew out from the back of Stanley's car.

"What did you say, Stanley?" Joan asked into the phone. "There was some kind of interference."

Stanley looked around the car. "Hold on. I'll turn down the radio."

He reached for a knob on the dashboard that he thought was the radio. However, it was the cigarette lighter. He fiddled with it for a second. Then he pulled it out of the dashboard.

"Oops."

He shrugged and tossed the lighter out the window. The glowing-hot lighter bounced onto the gasoline-soaked road. The gas burst into flames. The fire began running down the street along the trail of gas behind the car.

The soldiers in the Jeep were still following Stanley. They saw the fast-moving fire whipping up the street right toward them. The driver screamed and turned the steering wheel. The Jeep veered off the road and crashed into a ditch. The soldiers were thrown out onto the ground. The Jeep exploded.

Stanley continued driving down the road. He was unaware of what had happened on the street behind him.

Back at the Stupids' house, Joan finished talking to Stanley and hung up the phone. She turned to the children with a big smile. "Good news, kids. Your father's all right and he's on his way home!"

Buster shouted happily. "All right!"

Petunia was pacing back and forth. She was thinking. "It's been a very strange day, Mom. Very strange. And it makes me wonder." She stopped pacing and stared at her mother. "Is there something about Dad that you're not telling us? Something about his past that would help explain what's going on here?"

Joan bit her lip. She looked down at the curious faces of her kids staring up at her. "Children, I suppose you're old enough to know the truth. And the truth is that your father once worked inside the system."

"You mean . . . ?" Petunia began.

"That's right, Petunia," Joan answered. "Stanley Stupid was once a courier for the U.S. government."

Joan began to tell the story of Stanley's former life. "At first," Joan said, "it seemed like the perfect job. Every day brought new and fascinating challenges."

Back when Stanley was a letter carrier, he used to study carefully every letter that he pulled from his bag. It was amazing to him that nearly every letter had a different address. Day after day, it kept happening. He would peer at the address on the envelope and compare it with the numbers painted on the curb. He leaned down and dropped the letters into a grate in the street next to the curb address—a sewer grate. He moved down the street, slipping letters into any slot that was near the address on the curb—into the lunch box of a construction worker sitting on the curb, a schoolboy's backpack, a wood chipper that tore the letters into shreds and blew the little pieces into the air.

Joan continued to tell the children the story. "Then, one day, your father discovered something."

That day years ago, Stanley was sorting mail in the post office. Suddenly he saw something suspicious on an envelope. "That's odd," he said. He continued to sort mail. But he kept seeing the same strange problem. He gathered up a pile of envelopes and marched into his boss's office.

His boss saw Stanley and sighed heavily. "What is it now, Stanley?"

"Something very strange, sir," Stanley said. He dumped the armload of letters onto his boss's desk. "It seems that an enormous amount of letters are being delivered to someone named *Sender*." He held up one of the envelopes. It was stamped RETURN TO SENDER.

Stanley eyed his boss. "Who is this Sender, and what is he doing with other people's mail? I think this deserves a full-scale investigation."

The boss just stared at Stanley with his mouth open. Then he smacked himself on the forehead in disbelief.

Joan finished her story by saying, "The next day, your father was fired. They never told him why."

Buster said, "But of course—he knew too much!"

Petunia nodded wisely. "And my instinct tells me we haven't seen the last of Mr. Sender."

Meanwhile, at the colonel's headquarters, bad news was pouring in. The colonel sat behind his desk. He picked up the phone when it rang. He knew it was a call about the mission to eliminate Stanley Stupid.

"Is the target neutralized?" he asked.

On the other end of the line was the lieutenant. He sounded a little nervous. "I'm afraid not, sir. It seems the enemy repelled our assault team with extreme defensive aggression, in a blowing-up-their-car manner, sir."

The colonel nodded. "So he has some combat skills to back up his bravado. Who do we have from Special Operations?"

The lieutenant checked his files and said, "McClellan trained with the SOF, sir."

"Give him the assignment," the colonel ordered. "Let's see how our friend handles a veteran assassin."

A little later, Stanley pulled into a gas station. He was still on his way home in the colonel's car, but the gas tank was near empty. He honked the horn for the attendant.

He didn't notice a gray van pulling up to the pumps behind him. Driving the van was the lieutenant. Sitting next to him was a mean-looking soldier. The man was a trained Special Operations Forces expert. In his hands ordinary objects became lethal weapons. He had probably killed men with rubber bands and salt shakers.

The lieutenant watched Stanley get out of the car. The lieutenant looked at the Special Operations soldier. "Ready?"

"Ready," the soldier responded quietly. He flexed his hand and a knife blade clicked out of his wristband. "It's high time I got myself another tattoo." He held up his muscled forearm. It was covered with rows of tattooed skulls—one for each person he had assassinated!

The lieutenant eyed the skull tattoos. "Just make sure you do it clean. We can't afford to leave a trail of clues."

The Special Ops man smiled at him coldly. He pulled out a bottle of chloroform to knock Stanley unconscious. "Don't worry. He'll never know what hit him."

Stanley stood by the car as the young gas station attendant trotted up. The attendant looked at Stanley's car. He saw the bullet hole. He pointed to it and said, "Did you know you've got a hole in your fuel tank, sir?"

"Yes, son," Stanley answered without looking. "That's how you get the gas in it." He patted the young man on the shoulder. "Now why don't you top her off. I'm going to freshen up."

Stanley walked across the parking lot. There were two machines, labeled AIR and WATER. He picked up the water hose and sprayed himself in the face. Then he took the high-pressure air hose and started blowing himself dry. He hummed happily as if he were using a hair dryer at home.

Stanley didn't see the Special Ops soldier creeping up behind him. The soldier opened the chloroform bottle and poured some liquid onto a rag. He held up the rag, ready to place it over Stanley's mouth and nose and knock him out. However, as the soldier reached forward, a blast from the air hose blew the rag out of his hand. It flew back into his mouth.

The attendant yelled to Stanley, "All done, sir!"

"Super," Stanley said. He put away the air hose and started back to his car.

The soldier staggered backward. The chloroform was knocking him out. He fell onto a huge stack of large tractor tires. The tires toppled over and buried the soldier.

Stanley paid the attendant. "Thank you for the excellent service, young man." He got into his car and drove away.

The Special Ops soldier spit out the chloroform rag. He shook his head, trying to wake up. He sat up among the tires. He used his right hand to push himself up. When he did, the knife blade clicked out of his wristband and punctured one of the large rubber tires.

In the van, the lieutenant heard the loud *bang* as the tire exploded. He watched the Special Ops soldier fly through the air like a missile. The lieutenant shook his head and let out a sigh.

He picked up the phone and punched buttons. "Hello, Joe's Tattoo Parlor? Cancel the two o'clock appointment." Then he called the colonel.

The colonel answered in his usual gruff voice. "Well?"

"I'm afraid it's bad news," the lieutenant said.

The colonel paused. Then he said with disbelief, "Don't tell me he took out McClellan too?"

"It's uncanny, sir," the lieutenant answered. "I've watched him dispatch assailants effortlessly, with techniques that defy description."

The colonel asked, "Who's our explosives expert?"

"That would be Martinez, sir."

"Give him the assignment and give him everything he needs to pull it off," the colonel ordered. "I want it done surgical and I want it done now." He was angry. "For God's sake, we're military men. Killing people is supposed to be our job."

Stanley hummed happily as he headed toward home. He didn't notice a military motorcycle pulling up beside him. The motorcycle had a sidecar attached. Martinez, the explosives expert, rode in the sidecar. He was holding a bomb. He reached out as the two vehicles sped along the road and stuck the bomb into the bottom of the car. He signaled to the motorcycle driver. The motorcycle veered off and sped away.

Stanley heard a buzzing sound. A bug flew

around his face. He swatted at it. "Shoo! Get out of here." *Buzz. Buzz.* "Go on, leave me alone."

Then a bee landed on the steering wheel. Stanley jumped a little. "What are you trying to do, you darned bee? Can't you see I'm trying to drive?"

Stanley gasped in terror. He remembered what Joan had warned him about. "Oh my God—the drive bee!"

The bee started buzzing around Stanley's head again. Stanley pulled off one of his sneakers and swatted at the insect. "Fight, Stanley, fight for your life!"

Stanley swerved the car off the road. He hit the brakes in a shower of dirt and dust. He threw open the door and chased the bee out. He kept swatting at it. Finally he cornered the dangerous bug on the front bumper of the car.

He glared at the bee. "The tables have turned. The hunter becomes the hunted!"

He slammed the shoe down on the bumper. Just then the bomb exploded. The car blew up in a thundering flash of fire and smoke.

In the distance, Martinez and another soldier stood beside the army motorcycle. They were watching the explosion through binoculars. They nodded with satisfaction and said, "Mission accomplished. No one could have survived that blast." They got on the motorcycle and drove away.

But as the smoke cleared, Stanley stood there. He was still bent over, holding the shoe. He was black and smoking from the explosion. The car's bumper and front grille were still there, the only things left of the car. Stanley looked at the shoe in his hand. He was amazed.

He said, "Now *that* is a well-made shoe."

A short time later, a taxicab pulled up on the Stupids' street. Stanley got out of the cab and paid the driver. He didn't notice that he paid too much. "Here's your fare. And a little for yourself."

"Thank you, sir," the driver said. "What's the occasion?"

Stanley answered, "No occasion, driver. It's just good to be home."

As the cab drove away, Stanley stepped onto the lawn. He was overcome by emotion—the joy of returning home. He knelt down and picked some grass. He felt the lovely green blades between his fingers.

"Home," he said. "You never know how much it means to you until you go away."

Across the lawn, the door opened and Stanley's neighbor stepped out onto the porch. "What are you doing to my grass?" he asked Stanley.

"Buster?" Stanley squinted at the distant figure. "Is that you?" He could see the figure was an adult. "Have I been away so long?"

The neighbor said, "You live next door, Stanley."

"Please, call me Dad . . . ," Stanley said.

From Stanley's house next door, Buster saw his father and shouted, "Dad!"

Stanley saw his son come out of the house next door. "This day just gets stranger and stranger."

The Search for the Evil Mr. Sender

Stanley paced across the living room while Joan and the kids watched him. He thought deeply about what had been happening to his family. And he was beginning to have some ideas.

"We find ourselves today at the center of a puzzle," Stanley proclaimed. "At first, all is confusion. But as the pieces are fit together, patterns emerge, and before long we see the sinister face of conspiracy."

He tacked a piece of paper to the wall. Then he wrote the word *Sender* on the paper and circled it. "And it all begins with a man named Mr. Sender . . ."

Stanley started to explain his theory about the events. He wove a complicated tale that began with a tall, dark, evil archvillain named Mr. Sender. Sender sat on a throne deep within his villain headquarters.

He contemplated his evil deeds. He was surrounded by treasure chests labeled SENDER. They were brimming over with mail. His servants brought in more chests full of mail. He picked a letter out of a nearby chest.

"Letters," he said evilly. He ran his fingers over the envelope. "Easier to open than pistachios." He pulled out a silver letter opener and sliced open the envelope. He removed the letter inside and threw the envelope aside. "And what's inside is more delicious."

He unfolded the letter and began to read. " 'If you still love me, Sally, tie a yellow ribbon 'round the old oak tree.' " He chuckled to himself and said, "I'm afraid the only thing hanging from the old oak tree will be you. . . ." He read the signature on the letter. " '. . . Bob.' " He tore the letter in half and tossed it over his shoulder.

Sender grabbed a handful of letters and smiled. "Poor Jenny Miller . . ." He threw the envelopes off to the side. "No one's coming to her wedding!" He gathered up another bundle of letters. "And Grandma Jensen didn't pay her bills again this month." He tore them to shreds. "Time to put her in a home!"

In Stanley's story, the police officer who had given Petunia and Buster a ride home from the police station entered the headquarters of Mr. Sender. He stood in front of the evil genius and said, "This postal ploy of yours is the most evil caper of our age, Mr. Sender. How will you ever top yourself?"

Sender smiled. "With a crime so unthinkable no one has ever dared to attempt it—to rob an entire nation of its garbage!"

The police officer couldn't believe his ears. "Garbage! The one resource no one ever thinks to protect!" It was an amazing scheme.

Mr. Sender leaned forward on his throne. He reached out his hand, evil fingers spread. "And yet without it, every trash compactor, plastic bag, and Dumpster in America will be useless. Desperate men with empty wastebaskets will roam the streets! Panic and chaos will rule the land! The precious balance of civilization will be destroyed!" He closed his hand into a fist. Then he said in a quiet, sinister voice, "And the world will come begging for my mercy."

Sender looked at the police officer and commanded, "Your job is to kidnap anyone who discovers my diabolical plan. Including children."

Stanley Stupid took a deep breath and continued.

Neither Mr. Sender nor the police officer knew that at that moment a waiter named Johnson from a Chinese restaurant was listening at the window. Johnson was shocked by the sheer horror of Sender's plan. He said, "This fiendishness must be stopped!" The waiter ran to his bike and pedaled off.

Soon Johnson was in the kitchen of his restaurant, talking to another waiter. The second waiter was arguing. "It's not our battle to fight, Johnson. We've got enough trouble getting soy sauce into these tiny packets." He held up a fistful of little plastic packs.

Johnson said, "Maybe we can't stop Sender. But I know someone who can. A bright young man I worked with in the postal service . . ."

Meanwhile, downtown at the *Daily Times* building, Mr. Sender was giving orders to more of his lackeys. He stood with the two reporters in front of their computer.

Sender said, "Your job is to distract the public by continuing to print articles unrelated to my plan."

The first reporter nodded. Then he said, "As long as no one breaks into our computer and gets the real story."

Sender stared at him. "Have you posted guards out front?"

The second reporter said, "Only the best." He pointed out the window. Down the street were the crossing guard and the meter maid. The two looked up at the window and gave the reporter a thumbs-up signal.

Mr. Sender then called some of his other minions—local garbage collectors. The garbage collectors sat on their truck at the landfill. They had a cellular phone. "No one suspects a thing, Mr. Sender." They looked around. The only thing nearby, other than garbage, was a tiny bush. "Unless that bush has ears." The garbage collectors started laughing.

As they laughed, they couldn't hear Stanley's voice coming from the bush. "The joke's on you, my friends." It was a camouflage job worthy of a master spy.

The next day at Sender's villain headquarters, the police officer raced in. He was upset as he reported to his evil master. "Bad news, sir. Stanley Stupid has discovered our secret!"

Mr. Sender sat up on his throne, a diabolical gleam in his eye. "Stanley Stupid." He rubbed his hands together. "At last, a foe worthy of matching wits with." He glared at the police officer and said, "Release the drive bee!"

The police officer grabbed a crank handle. With a fiendish grin he began to turn it. A vault creaked open on the wall. Then the police officer reached into the vault and seized a lever. He tugged it. Gears and wheels began to grind. From deep within the vault, a platform emerged. There was a glass jar sitting on it. Inside the jar was a single, evil killer bee!

Stanley stood in the living room. He paused in his story and turned to his family. "So you see, it all begins with Mr. Sender."

Petunia exclaimed, "Wow, Dad!"

"Yeah, wow!" Buster said.

Joan added, "The police are against us. And obviously we can't go to the press. What are we going to do, Stanley?"

Stanley said, "The only thing we can do, Joan. We've got to take on Sender ourselves." He continued to pace and think. "Oh, it won't be easy finding him. Scouring the countryside for microscopic clues, following trails long since cold, sensing him always nearby, yet somehow maddeningly beyond our grasp!"

Petunia had the phone book open on her lap. "Hey, there's a Charles Sender listed right here in the phone book."

Stanley declared, "The manhunt begins!"

The Stupids rushed out of the house. They all piled into the station wagon. Stanley tried to start the car, but he couldn't. He kept trying to turn the starter. However, he didn't have the keys.

He shouted, "The car won't start!"

Kitty the dog trotted up to the car. He had the keys in his mouth. He shook his head, jangling the keys. No one noticed him.

Buster leaned over the back of the front seat. "Maybe the battery's dead."

Joan said, "It was perfectly healthy this afternoon."

Stanley leapt out of the car. "Then there may still be life in it. I'd better give it mouth-to-mouth." The dog cleared his throat. Stanley stepped past the dog. "Not now, Kitty. I've got a battery to revive!"

Stanley threw up the hood. He took a deep breath. Then he put his mouth on the car battery. Suddenly he snapped back. Sparks of electricity shot off his head.

"Wait a second," Stanley began. "What am I doing?" He took a new look, a look of intelligence and wisdom and awareness. "I've cooked up an insane conspiracy theory and put myself in the middle of an illegal weapons sale among some of the world's most dangerous men. I'm risking my life and the lives of my family in a scheme that makes absolutely no sense at all!"

The electricity began to fade from his head. "Insight fading . . . Must remember . . . not to go forward with this. . . ."

Joan stuck her head out the window. "What is it, Stanley? What are you supposed to remember?"

"Uh . . ." The last spark zipped off Stanley's head. He thought for a second. Then he shrugged. "I don't know."

The old Stanley Stupid returned. He smiled with gusto. "Now let's go, everybody. We've got a job to do!"

The dog tossed Stanley the keys. Stanley jumped into the car and started the engine. The Stupids backed out of the driveway and sped off down the street.

The Stupids' station wagon screeched into the parking lot of the Natural History Museum. There was a sign out front that read CLOSED TODAY.

Joan looked at the old, dark building. "You're sure this is the place?"

Stanley said, "Oh yes. When I called Sender's *home,* his *wife* said he *worked* here."

Joan nodded. "A likely story."

The Stupids got out of the car. Stanley gathered them around. "Joan, you and Buster search this end of the building. Petunia and I will take this side. And remember, everybody, use your heads."

Joan and Buster wandered along one side of the building. They found a window that was open just a crack. Joan managed to shove the window open a little more. Buster boosted his mom up. Joan grunted and groaned, struggling to climb through the window. She finally made it.

Buster tried to climb in after her. But he was a little too small. He couldn't quite make it. Joan came out of a nearby door and walked up behind her son. She gave him a push. Buster climbed inside.

Joan then tried to climb in after him. She got stuck in the window. Buster came out of the door and walked back to the window. He gave his mother a push and she fell into the museum. Then Buster climbed up. Joan reached out and grabbed him. She pulled him inside. They brushed themselves off and shook hands. More Stupid teamwork!

Joan and Buster tiptoed down the dark halls of the museum. Then Joan saw a door labeled CHARLES SENDER—CURATOR.

"I've found his headquarters!" Joan called to Buster.

But Buster had wandered into another room, the Hall of Science. In the large room was a display of a giant microscope, a large turbine engine, and a big DNA molecule. Buster stared at the collection of

49

strange equipment. He shouted to his mom, "And I've stumbled upon his fiendish laboratory!"

Meanwhile, Stanley and Petunia were sneaking around another part of the museum. They came to a door. They didn't see the sign over the door— PLANETARIUM. Petunia tried the handle.

"Dad!" she said. "This door is unlocked."

"Good work, Petunia."

They walked into the planetarium. Stanley said, "Careful, Petunia. One false move and we could end up dead."

The door swung shut behind them. The room was very dark.

"Dad?" Petunia called out.

"Petunia?"

Petunia's voice was quivering. "Everything's gone dark. I can't see a thing!"

Stanley said, "Oh my God! It's happened!"

"We're dead!" Petunia cried.

"I knew it!"

Petunia stumbled through the darkness. She ran into a big switch. It shifted from OFF to ON. The planetarium machinery started up. The big projector in the middle of the room lit up and cast images of stars, galaxies, and comets on the circular ceiling. The stars streaked across the fake sky. Constellations rose and set in minutes. Planets and the moon moved overhead.

Stanley said, "So this is heaven."

Petunia looked around. "It's quite lovely, really."

Stanley nodded in agreement. But he said, "Still, I miss the earth."

They strolled toward the center of the room. There was a large model of the solar system. The planets were revolving around a big plastic sun in the center.

"Funny, isn't it?" Stanley mused. "One minute you're tracking down the head of a global conspiracy and the next minute—*poof*! It's over. Really puts things in perspective."

Petunia watched the planets and their moons swirl around. "You know who I miss the most? Mom and Buster."

Stanley comforted her. "Don't worry, honey. They'll be here soon enough, the way your mother drives."

Suddenly they heard footsteps. Lloyd, the museum janitor, stepped into the planetarium and peered into the dimness.

"Hello?" he called. "Somebody in here?"

Petunia grabbed Stanley's arm. "Dad, someone's coming. Do you think . . . ?"

"Yes, Petunia," Stanley answered with excitement. "It's time to meet our Creator."

Lloyd crossed the dim planetarium. He was carrying a mop and a bucket.

Stanley raised his arms and prayed, "Hail to Thee, O Lord."

The janitor pointed to the name tag on his shirt. "Actually, it's pronounced Lloyd."

Stanley stared at the name tag in amazement. "All these years we've been saying it wrong."

At the same time, Joan was searching Mr. Sender's office. Joan picked up a photograph of a man in a theme park holding a big bunch of balloons. He was smiling cheerfully.

She stared at the picture. "So this is the face of evil."

Then she found his appointment book and calendar on his desk. She flipped through the pages. "And *this* is the diary of his twisted schemes." She stuffed the book into her pocket.

Across the hall, Buster was still wandering through the Hall of Science. He was studying a long time line of world history that was painted on the wall. It was fascinating. "Dates . . . numbers . . . years . . ." Then the time line crossed an elevator. The doors were open. Buster stopped. "What in the world?"

Joan scurried up beside him. "Come on, Buster. I've found out where Sender's going next!"

Buster said, "Just a minute, Mom. I've discovered a mysterious little room here." He pointed to the old-fashioned floor dial over the elevator. It had an arrow that slid along a scale of numbers as the elevator moved up and down. "There's a strange-looking clock over the top of it."

Buster stepped inside the elevator. He saw the rows of buttons on the wall. "And a control panel inside full of numbers. One would almost think it was some kind of . . . time machine." He punched some buttons. The elevator began to close.

He looked out in terror. "Mom, help!"

Joan shouted, "Buster, no!"

She dived into the elevator. The doors slid shut behind her.

Joan stood up. She and Buster were beginning to panic. "What buttons did you press?" she asked her son.

"I don't know!" Buster said frantically. "Just a bunch of random numbers and the letters BC . . ."

Joan gasped. "Oh my God."

The elevator doors opened. They were staring into a large room full of dinosaurs and Ice Age animals like mammoths and giant sloths.

Joan looked at the herd of unmoving creatures. The realization hit her like a thunderbolt. "We've traveled back to the age of the dinosaurs."

Back in the planetarium, Stanley and Petunia were talking to Lloyd, the janitor. But they didn't know he was a janitor. Lloyd was just happy that someone was taking time to talk to him. It didn't happen very often.

Petunia said, "It's just so amazing to meet you at last."

The janitor smiled. "Well, thank you. It sure is nice to meet someone who appreciates the work I do."

Stanley said, "Appreciate it? Why, you're the one who takes care of the entire universe!"

Lloyd pointed at the model solar system. "You know it takes me half an hour sometimes just to clean Saturn? But you'd be surprised how little thanks I get for it. Most people don't even know I exist."

Petunia nodded wisely. "That's the modern world for you."

Joan and Buster crept through the Jurassic era and the Ice Age. They looked up at the giant, creepy animals that posed all around them. Joan and Buster were surrounded by shadowy dinosaurs and monstrous mammals who had been frozen as they attacked weaker creatures.

Buster said, "This is the single most fantastic journey in the history of the world."

Joan whispered, "Keep your voice down, son. If one of these things wakes up, we're in real trouble."

Buster shouted, "Mom, look! The cave of some prehistoric peoples."

He stepped into a display of cave dwellers. A fake family of Neanderthals sat around a fake fire. The cave was covered with paintings of bison and antelopes. Buster reached down between two cave dwellers and picked up a stone axe. It was amazingly light.

Buster said, "Their tools seem to be fashioned from some kind of primitive Styrofoam."

Joan cautioned him. "We've got to be careful. The

slightest disturbance to this ancient world could affect the entire course of history."

Buster suddenly got an idea. His eyes lit up. "Yes. The entire course of history . . ."

He took a pen out of his pocket. He wrote the word *Buster* on the cave wall.

Joan turned and saw him defacing the Neanderthals' home. "What are you doing?"

"Just imagine," Buster said. "My name is now the first word ever written! This rock will be the most sacred mystery on earth!"

Joan approached her son. "Buster, snap out of it!"

Buster stared off into space. He was overcome by the scope of his actions. "When people learn to read, I'll be worshiped! Nations will rise and fall in my name! Life on earth will be nothing more than a footnote to Buster!"

Joan grabbed him by the arm. She started dragging him back to the elevator. "We've got to get out of here!"

How to Break into Television 5

Stanley and Petunia were still in the planetarium. And they still thought they were dead. And they were still talking to Lloyd the janitor. And they still didn't know he was Lloyd the janitor.

Stanley said, "Not to be disrespectful, but . . ." He shrugged and smiled a little. "I feel that perhaps we've come here too early."

Lloyd agreed. "I'll say. The truth is, you two shouldn't be here at all."

Stanley got excited. Perhaps this meant a new lease on life for his daughter and him. "Do you mean . . . you're sending us back into the world?"

"I'm afraid so," the janitor replied. "Don't get me wrong. It's been a pleasure talking to you. But there's work to be done."

Stanley said, more to himself than anyone else,

"So our crusade against the world's injustice is important!"

Lloyd pointed across the planetarium. "Just head through the door marked EXIT. That'll take you back to where you parked your car."

Stanley turned to his daughter. "Did you hear that, Petunia? We're getting a second chance!"

Petunia shouted, "Hooray!"

Then she stood on tiptoe and kissed Lloyd the janitor on the cheek. "Do you have any final words for us before we go?" she asked.

Lloyd thought for a second. Then, in a kindly voice, he answered, "Well, if you want to make my job easier, remember to throw your gum in the trash when you're done chewing it. I spend a huge amount of my time cleaning up gum."

"So long as we live, we will fight that wrong," Stanley promised.

Stanley took Petunia's hand. They walked together to the EXIT door. They pushed it open and passed from the darkness into the light of a wonderful new day.

Petunia gazed around her at the sunny world. "Ah, life! How I've missed it!"

"Blessed is the Lloyd," Stanley said reverently.

Back inside the museum, Joan dragged Buster into the elevator. She turned to the control panel and stared at it. She hit some numbered buttons and then the letters AD. She figured this would at least get her closer to the present.

"We must get back to our own time!" she said as she pressed buttons madly.

The elevator doors closed. When they opened again, she and Buster saw the lobby of the museum. Just as they had left it! They were home!

They staggered out of the elevator. They were drained by what they thought had been an amazing trip through time.

Buster shook his head as if he were coming out of a trance. "Sorry, Mom. I sort of went mad with power back there."

Joan said, "Well, the important thing is, we made it." She took the Styrofoam axe away from Buster. "And now to make sure this diabolical machine is never used again."

She leapt back into the elevator and began bashing the walls with the fake axe. She hacked and hacked. Then she paused to catch her breath. There was no damage to the elevator. But her axe was pulverized. Little bits of Styrofoam floated around her.

"It didn't leave a scratch," she said in awe.

Buster ran his hand along the inside of the elevator. "What kind of space age materials is this thing made of?"

They hurried out of the museum. Across the parking lot, they saw Stanley and Petunia waiting impatiently.

Joan called out, "Stanley! Petunia!"

Stanley rushed toward his wife. "You made it!"

They embraced in the parking lot.

Joan asked, "Are you all right? How did it go in there?"

Stanley said, "It was a remarkable twenty minutes, Joan. We died, went to heaven, met God, and were brought back to life." He shook his head. "But still no sign of Sender. What happened to you?"

Joan answered, "We traveled through time to the age of the dinosaurs and Buster established himself as the most important and mysterious figure in history."

Stanley scowled at his son. "Buster!"

"Sorry, Dad." Buster offered a thin smile and looked at the ground.

Joan continued, "And more importantly, we found this."

She pulled Charles Sender's appointment book out of her pocket. She handed it to Stanley. He thumbed through it curiously.

Stanley said, "Numbers, names, dates, times. Wait a minute. There's an entry in here for today!" He read from the page. "Channel Three news. One o'clock."

Petunia said, "We passed the Channel Three news station on the way here."

Buster looked at his watch. "And it's almost one now!"

Joan exclaimed, "The trail is still fresh!"

"Let's go!" shouted Stanley.

* * *

Nearby, the lieutenant was driving the colonel in another one of their cars. The colonel had just hung up the car phone.

He said, "That was our banker in Bern." The colonel was setting up a secret Swiss bank account. "Payments will be transferred to us upon delivery of the hardware." He looked at his watch. "In approximately *t*-minus four hours."

The lieutenant nodded and smiled a little. "Then it's as good as done. Nothing imaginable can stop us now."

Just then the Stupids' station wagon passed them going in the opposite direction. Stanley recognized the colonel. He honked the horn and waved at the two men as he went past.

The lieutenant and the colonel looked at each other.

"That's impossible!" the lieutenant said. "We killed that man yesterday!"

The colonel glared at his junior officer. "Well, we'd better have him killed again. Our future is in his hands."

The Channel 3 news station was in a skyscraper in the downtown area. Out front, important people in the worlds of news and entertainment were coming and going. One well-dressed woman got into her fancy car. She paused to light a cigarette.

Suddenly the Stupids' station wagon swerved into the space in front of her. It banged against the front

"I've got a feeling something special's going to happen today,"
says Joan. Time for the Stupids to rise and shine . . .

. . . and shower!

Someone has stolen the Stupids' garbage again. And Stanley won't rest until he's brought the thief to justice!

Mom and Dad *missing*? Buster and Petunia study the take-out menu left near their front door. What could it mean?

Stanley's found his missing garbage! Cleverly disguised, he moves closer to the action at the dump.

To look like a bush, you must think like a bush.

"Something fishy is going on around here. Frankly, our lives may be in danger," says Stanley.

"Is that you, Mom?" Petunia and Buster meet up with their mother at the offices of the *Daily Times* . . .

. . . and soon their search for clues is smoking!

Back at home, Stanley explains his theory of the sinister plot that's under way . . .

. . . as Joan, Petunia, and Buster listen spellbound.

This museum isn't boring! The Stupids search for the mysterious Mr. Sender . . .

. . . travel through time . . .

. . . and survive death!

Who *is* this man? And why is he here? wonders the host of the *Debbie* show.

The colonel catches up to Stanley, but no one can stop the Stupids now! They're off to the big showdown!

Home at last. Time to relax, barbecue, and celebrate saving the world. And the Stupids do just that, thanks to the quick-thinking family cat and dog!

of her car. The air bag whooshed out of the car's steering wheel. When the air bag touched the glowing tip of the woman's cigarette, it exploded—*bang!*

Stanley leapt from the station wagon. "We're here!" The Stupids all hurried into the building.

The woman in the fancy car stared at them silently. Her head was smoking. Her hair was frizzed out in every direction.

The lobby of the Channel 3 building was decorated with posters of the shows that were taped there. One poster was for the evening news. Another advertised a talk show called *The Late at Night Show*. And another poster publicized *Debbie*, a popular daytime talk show for people whose problems evidently could be solved only if the sufferers appeared on television.

Stanley stopped in the middle of the lobby. He gathered his family in a huddle and said, "Somewhere in this building is the man we're looking for. Let's find him—before he finds us!"

Stanley and Buster went off in one direction. Joan and Petunia raced off in another.

In a studio not far away, Charles Sender was doing a live interview on the *One O'Clock News*.

The attractive, well-dressed anchorwoman spoke into the camera. "Good news today for culture buffs. A new exhibit arrives at the Museum of Natural History, and here to tell us about the highlights is the museum director, Charles Sender."

Mr. Sender sat next to her. He was a small, cheerful man—hardly a threat to world peace at all.

Sender said, "Well, the new acquisition includes a number of lively pieces, but my favorite is a set of marvelously preserved Mesopotamian statues known collectively as . . ." He held up a photograph of a group of strange, scary statues. "The Lords of the Underworld."

The anchorwoman said, "Now, I understand it's exhibits like this that have given our museum its most profitable year ever. You must be a very sought-after curator."

Sender chuckled and blushed. "Oh, yes. Sometimes I feel like a hunted man."

Just then Stanley and Buster passed right by the news set. They didn't see Sender and they kept going.

Joan and Petunia moved cautiously down a hallway. They looked around them, searching for signs of the Sender.

Joan said, "Try your best to blend in, Petunia. Remember, we can't afford to get caught."

Two secretaries walked by, laughing together. Joan and Petunia laughed together too, trying to imitate them. Then a producer went past, muttering angrily over his show's ratings. Joan and Petunia changed their tones suddenly and started muttering angrily over some show's ratings.

Then a young delivery boy stopped them. He was

carrying a package. He looked upset and was obviously in a great hurry. "Excuse me. I'm looking for the set of *The Late at Night Show* . . ."

Joan tried to imitate him. "Excuse *me. I'm* looking for the set of *The Late at Night Show*."

The delivery boy continued. "I'm supposed to make a delivery there."

Joan said, *"I'm* supposed to make a delivery there."

The delivery boy took a deep breath of relief. "Lady, you may have just saved my job!" He handed his package to Joan. "If you could give this to Doug the stagehand, I would be so grateful. He's a big fat guy, you can't miss him. Here . . ." He pulled a backstage pass off his own shirt and pinned it to Joan's. "This'll get you backstage. I really appreciate this!"

As the delivery boy hurried off, Joan and Petunia continued sneaking down the hall. They reached some double doors that had a sign reading AUTHORIZED PERSONS ONLY. There was a guard standing there too. He was turning people away from the door.

"I'm sorry," the guard told the people, "but they're taping a show now. Absolutely no one comes through without authorization."

Then the guard saw Joan's backstage pass. He waved her and Petunia through. "Right this way, ma'am."

Stanley and Buster were wandering around.

Stanley said, "Keep your eyes peeled for anything

unusual, son. Where there's deviance, Mr. Sender can't be far away. Just watch for the slightest sign of perversion."

Buster looked through an open door and saw something weird. "Dad!" He pointed into the room. "They're putting makeup on men in here."

"Bull's-eye," said Stanley.

Stanley and Buster entered the makeup room. A line of chairs stood in front of a big mirror. Three men and three women sat in the chairs with towels wrapped around their necks. There were several women in the room applying makeup to the men's faces.

Right behind Stanley and Buster, another man leaned into the makeup room. He had a badge that read ASSISTANT DIRECTOR. He asked, "Are they ready?"

One of the makeup ladies said, "Ready when you are."

The assistant director clapped his hands. "Then let's go, everyone. We're on."

The six people stood up and removed the towels. They moved out of the makeup room in a line. Stanley got caught in the rush and he was hustled along with the crowd. He wasn't sure where he was going.

On the stage of *The Late at Night Show*, a glamorous movie actress was being interviewed by the host of the show. She was saying, "You know, people seem to think it's easy being a celebrity. But when they canceled my series, *Beach Detective*, I was absolutely devastated."

The APPLAUSE sign above the stage lit up. The audience clapped loudly. The actress and the host looked around, a little confused. Normally someone being devastated wasn't cause for applause.

Backstage, Petunia was flipping the switch that controlled the APPLAUSE sign. She whispered, "Psst— Mom! I can't get this light switch to work."

Joan was setting the package down on a table. "Just a moment, dear." She took a large piece of paper and wrote, *"Give it to the fat guy."* Then she walked over to Petunia. "Now let's have a look."

When Joan turned away, a stagehand collected several large pieces of paper from the table. One of them was the piece that Joan had written on. They were cue cards for the host of *The Late at Night Show.*

Back onstage, the actress was getting mad. All the weirdly timed applause was annoying her. She yelled at the audience, "Well, maybe you'd all be happier if there *was* no prime-time television. You could spend every night reading books together."

The APPLAUSE sign came on again. The audience clapped. The angry actress stood up and stormed off the set.

The host tried to cover. "Well. My next guest is a world-class French chef." He squinted to see the cue card. "So, stay tuned, everyone, and let's give it to the fat guy."

A large chef dressed in white and wearing a big

puffy white hat burst through the curtains. Insulted, he began to yell at the host in French. The APPLAUSE sign came on. The audience clapped. The host was totally confused.

Stanley was sitting on a stage with six people from the makeup room. He was very nervous. Buster stood off to the side, watching anxiously.

The assistant director stood behind the camera. He called out, "Let's settle down, everybody! We're on in five, four, three . . ."

The theme music to the *Debbie* show came on and the audience applauded. The host of the show, Debbie, appeared. She held a microphone and spoke to the audience.

"Have you ever thought you came from an unusual family?" Many people in the audience nodded. Debbie continued. "Well, after you've met my guests today, you may want to adjust your standards."

Debbie walked over to the first man onstage. He leaned to her microphone and said, "I divorced my wife in order to date her sister."

The next guest, a woman, said, "I've been engaged to three of my cousins."

Another woman guest said, "I married a Siamese twin."

Then Debbie put the microphone in front of Stanley. He twitched and looked around nervously. Everyone in the studio audience was staring at him.

"I . . ." He thought. "Uh, well, to tell the truth, I . . ."

There was a tense silence in the studio. Debbie looked at him, waiting for his story. Stanley swallowed hard. Then he thought of something.

"I'm my own grandpa," he said.

Debbie looked at him as if she didn't believe him. "You're your own grandpa?"

"That's right," Stanley said.

Debbie said, "Well, for those of us who've never heard of such a thing, maybe you could explain."

Stanley smiled. "Of course. It's quite simple, really." Then he began to sing.

> "Many, many years ago
> When I was twenty three
> I was married to a widow
> As pretty as can be.
> This widow had a grown-up
> daughter
> Who had hair of red.
> My father fell in love with her
> And soon they too were wed."

Debbie nodded. "Okay."
Stanley continued his song.

> "This made my dad my son-in-law
> And changed my very life,
> For my daughter was my mother

'Cause she was my father's wife.
To complicate the matter,
Even though it brought me joy,
I soon became the father
Of a bouncing baby boy."

Debbie said, "I see."

"My little baby then became
A brother-in-law to Dad
And so became my uncle,
Though it made me very sad,
For if he was my uncle
Then that also made him brother
Of the widow's grown-up daughter
Who of course was my stepmother."

Debbie suddenly realized where he was going.
"Which means that . . ."

"I'm my own grandpa!
I'm my own grandpa!
It sounds funny, I know,
But it really is so.
Oh, I'm my own grandpa!"

At the Reverend Wright's ministry, the assistant burst
into the reverend's office. He turned on the television.

"We've found him," the assistant reported.

"Where?" the Reverend Wright asked.

"There." The assistant pointed to the television, where Stanley was singing on the *Debbie* show.

The reverend jumped to his feet and grabbed his coat.

The assistant spoke up meekly. "Reverend, forgive me for saying so, but . . . I'm beginning to have doubts about this. It's strange, really, but something about that man really affects me." He looked at the image of Stanley singing on the screen. "There's a simplicity and innocence that I truly respond to . . ."

The Reverend Wright stared at him. The assistant shut up.

"Are you questioning me?" Wright asked. "*Are* you?"

The assistant was quiet for a second. Then he said, "No, Reverend."

The Reverend Wright strode out the door. The assistant followed him. But he looked very upset and disturbed.

Stanley continued to sing.

> *"Father's wife then had a son*
> *Who kept him on the run.*
> *And he became my grandchild*
> *For he was my daughter's son.*
> *My wife is now my mother's mother*
> *And it makes me blue . . .*

Because although she is my wife
She's my grandmother too.
If my wife is my grandmother
Then I am her grandchild.
And every time I think of it
It nearly drives me wild."

Debbie shook her head in disbelief. She said, in time to the song, "This has got to be the strangest thing I ever saw . . ."

Stanley sang on.

"As husband of my grandmother
I am my own grandpa
I'm my own grandpa!
I'm my own grandpa!
It sounds funny I know . . ."

"But it really is so," Debbie added.

"I'm my own grandpa!" Stanley finished.

Debbie turned to the audience. "Stay tuned, everyone. We'll be right back after this break."

A Stupid Hostage 6

Later, as Stanley and Buster left the studio, they turned the corner and saw Mr. Sender at the end of the hall. He was getting into an elevator. And he was shaking hands with the anchorwoman from the *One O'Clock News*.

She said, "Thanks again for coming to the station, Mr. Sender."

"Oh, it was a pleasure, I assure you," he replied.

Stanley shouted, "Sender. We meet at last!"

Sender waved pleasantly at Stanley as the elevator doors closed. "No time to talk, I'm afraid," Sender called out. "I've got to pick up the Lords of the Underworld."

The elevator door shut.

Stanley and Buster looked at each other.

Buster exclaimed, "The Lords of the Under-world?"

Stanley said, "Buster, I'm beginning to think we're on to something even bigger than we ever suspected."

"You mean . . . ?" Buster began.

Stanley nodded. "Yes, son. Sender may be in a league with—"

"Stanley!" Joan came rushing up the hall. "We just saw Sender leaving the building."

Petunia stood at a window. She was pointing down to the street. Many floors below, Sender got into a van from the museum and drove away.

Stanley said, "Joan, it seems we're involved in much more than just a criminal conspiracy to divert the mail and steal garbage. Unless I'm gravely mistaken, this is part of the final war between Good and Evil, the apocalyptic battle for men's and women's souls that heralds the end of the world!"

Just then the elevator door opened. The Reverend Wright stepped out. He was followed by two muscular henchmen. From where the Stupids were standing, the red arrow above the door shined through the reverend's white hair. It looked as if he had a sinister red halo.

Petunia screeched.

The Reverend Wright pointed at Stanley and threatened, "You've taken on a power far greater than you ever imagined, Stanley Stupid!"

The reverend's two henchmen grabbed Stanley and dragged him back into the elevator.

Joan and the kids tried to fight. Petunia bit someone in the shins. Buster tore at one of their jackets. But the henchmen were too strong. They shoved the other Stupids out of the elevator. The door closed on Stanley and the henchmen and a smiling Reverend Wright. Stanley was gone!

Petunia shouted, "Oh my God! Dad's been captured!"

Joan was trying to be rational. "Now wait a minute! We don't know for sure who those men were."

Buster said, "Don't we, Mom? *Don't* we?"

He raised his hand. He was holding a tag that he had ripped off the inside of one of the henchmen's coats. The tag read 100% SATIN.

Joan said in a terrified whisper, "One hundred percent Satan."

The three Stupids looked at each other, horror-stricken. Then they screamed at the top of their lungs.

In the parking lot, the henchmen stuffed Stanley into the backseat of the reverend's limousine. They climbed in after him. The assistant was back there too. The Reverend Wright climbed into the front passenger seat. The limo took off down the street.

Stanley said bravely, "So. It seems I've uncovered a little too much for my own good."

The reverend didn't look back. "You should have

known better than to cross a man like me, Mr. Stupid. It is written in the Good Book that whoever disturbs the house of a minister shall feel the wrath of heaven."

Stanley pulled Sender's appointment book out of his pocket. He said, "I was hoping I'd meet someone who knows a thing or two about the book."

He flipped through the book. He found a page that read, "Fund-raising dinner. Museum needs $$$."

"For instance," Stanley asked, "do you understand what it takes to make a true profit?"

Wright glared at Stanley. He said angrily, "I *am* a true prophet! And you'll learn to regret that kind of insolence!"

Stanley rolled his eyes. "Geez, I'm just asking some questions."

Then he turned to another section of the book. There was a list of names and times. Stanley asked, "What, for instance, is the meaning of John 4:20? Or Peter 6:25?"

The assistant was becoming interested now. He couldn't tell that Stanley was looking in an appointment book. He could just see that it was some kind of fancy leather-covered book. He assumed it was a Bible. So he pulled out his own Bible and turned to the Book of John, chapter 4, verse 20.

He read to himself. "Beware of the man who puts himself before the gospel."

Then he turned to the Book of Peter, chapter 6, verse 25.

He read again. "Repent before the hour of judgment comes."

He looked heavenward as he thought about those passages.

The other Stupids were following the limousine in their station wagon. Joan swerved through traffic, trying to keep the big car in sight.

Buster asked, "I wonder why the evil ones drive such a long car."

Joan said over her shoulder, "As I understand it, Buster, all the cars in hell are long. The parking spaces are very small, however, and valets who have sinned in life must try to park them for all eternity."

Buster and Petunia exchanged glances. They didn't quite understand that explanation.

In the backseat of the reverend's limousine, the assistant was whispering to Stanley. "And the truth is, well, lately I've been having doubts. Deep crises of belief. I feel as if the whole foundation of my faith is crumbling beneath me."

Stanley said, "Crumbling foundations, eh? Well, it is written in the book that a man will come to repair what is broken." Stanley glanced at a page in the book that referred to a repairman coming to do work at the museum.

The assistant asked, "Are you that man?"

Suddenly a military Jeep skidded to a halt in front of the limousine. It blocked the road. The limo driver slammed on the brakes. Then a second Jeep screeched to a halt behind the reverend's car.

Two soldiers leapt out of the Jeep. They raced to the back door of the limousine and threw it open. They pointed their guns inside.

One soldier said, "We'll take Mr. Stupid now, if you don't mind."

The soldiers pulled Stanley from the limousine. They hustled him up to the Jeep and tossed him in the back. Then both Jeeps pulled out and drove away.

The Reverend Wright fumed with anger. "So he has some pros on his side, does he? Well, I've got pros on my side too. And I've got a feeling mine are a lot tougher."

Glancing at the reverend, the assistant felt more doubtful than ever.

The Stupids swerved around the limo and kept chasing. They had seen the soldiers grab Stanley.

Buster said, "What is the U.S. Army doing with Dad? They're supposed to protect Americans."

Joan said, "So are the police, Buster. And they kidnap children."

The Stupids kept pursuing the Jeeps. Then they saw the vehicles pull into a military base. The Jeeps roared past the guard at the checkpoint with just a quick salute.

As the station wagon approached, the guard stepped out into the street and raised his hand. Joan braked. The Jeeps disappeared in the distance.

* * *

The two Jeeps ground to a stop in front of the colonel's headquarters. The two soldiers yanked Stanley out of the Jeep and dragged him inside. Two armed guards stood outside the headquarters. They nodded as the soldiers took Stanley in.

Soon he was seated in front of the colonel. Stanley was pleased to see him.

"Well, hello again," Stanley said cheerfully. "I appreciate you saving my hide back there. But you can tell your men, I really don't need an escort any longer—"

The colonel snapped, "You're a clever man, Mr. Stupid—if that really is your name. Too clever for your own good."

The two soldiers tied Stanley's hands.

Stanley was confused. He shouted, "Hey! What are you doing? We're on the same side here."

The colonel laughed. "And you play the innocent most convincingly."

Stanley looked at the colonel. "But I thought—"

"You thought you'd fool me into thinking you were dead. And then you'd catch me red-handed when I went to make the sale. A masterful bit of strategy. And you came dangerously close to pulling it off."

The lieutenant entered the room. "We'd better get going, sir. We're due at Warehouse Twenty-one in less than an hour."

Stanley said, "Warehouse Twenty-one . . ."

The colonel shook his head. "No use gathering intelligence now, my friend. Our little chess game is over."

The colonel nodded to one of the soldiers. The soldier pulled out his pistol and twisted a silencer onto the barrel.

The colonel walked to the door. He turned back to Stanley and said, "I hope you won't find the end game too unpleasant."

Back at the guard post, Joan was arguing with the armed guard. "But you've got to let us in there! It's an emergency!"

The guard stared with a blank face. He was polite but firm. "I'm sorry, ma'am. There's nothing I can do."

Joan backed the station wagon out of the entryway. Then she pulled over to the side of the road and parked.

"It's no use," she said in a depressed voice. "They won't let anyone onto that army base unless they're in the army."

Petunia said, "This is serious. Dad's in danger. We've got to think of something!"

Buster had an idea. "Wait a minute! What if we formed our *own* army?"

"To do that we'd have to form our own country," Petunia argued.

Joan joined in. "We could call it Stupidia, a sovereign nation, with its own laws, its own customs, its own government . . .''

Petunia said, "Mom, as mother of this household, your leadership has stood the test of time. I'd like to nominate you as president!"

Joan was always fair. She suggested, "And you can run a tough campaign against me!"

Buster declared, "Start the debates already! There isn't much time!"

Petunia lowered her eyebrows. She glared at her mother like a suspicious politician. "Mrs. Stupid, you claim to stand for family values—but isn't it true that your own daughter is running a bitter and merciless crusade against you, prodding, interrogating, and questioning the very integrity of your character?"

Joan glared back. "Well, if it's a smear campaign you want, why not let the people know that your own *mother* eats newspaper?"

With that, she grabbed a piece of newspaper. She crumpled it up and brought it toward her mouth.

Petunia shot back, "My mother learned that habit from *you*, Mrs. Stupid!"

Joan looked shocked. "Me? Why, I've never eaten a newspaper in my life!"

Buster interrupted. "And I'm afraid that's all the time we have." He handed pencils to Petunia and his mother. "To the polls, everyone!"

Stanley sat in the chair with his hands tied. The two soldiers stood over him. The soldier without the pistol looked nervous. He said, "Get this over with already, would you? This guy's already taken out three of our best."

The first soldier sneered. "Relax. His hands are tied, he's unarmed, I've got a gun on him, and there are two armed guards posted out front. There's no way he's getting out of here alive. Isn't that right, Mr. Stupid?"

Then the soldier spit a piece of gum on the ground. Stanley gasped. If Lloyd had been here, he would have been very angry. Stanley recalled the wise and thoughtful words of Lloyd: "Remember to throw your gum in the trash when you're done chewing it. I spend a huge amount of time cleaning up gum."

This made Stanley angrier than he had ever been in his life. He stood up and shouted, "In the name of the Lloyd!" With divinely inspired, superhuman strength, he tore apart the ropes around his wrists. He charged at the soldiers.

The soldiers jumped out of Stanley's way. He charged by them directly out a second-floor window.

There was a flagpole right outside the window. Thinking fast, Stanley grabbed the rope attached to the top of the flagpole. His weight began to take him down. On the ground, one of the guards stood next to the flagpole. His pants got caught in the rope as it whipped past. The guard was yanked off his feet and up the pole. Stanley went past him going down.

The soldiers leaned out of the colonel's window to

get a shot at Stanley. The guard came flying up the flagpole, and his feet smacked both soldiers on the chin and knocked them out.

When Stanley reached the ground, the second guard pointed his rifle at him. "All right! Put your hands up!" he commanded Stanley.

Stanley obeyed. But he let go of the rope. The first guard came whizzing down the flagpole, crashing on top of the second guard. Both of the guards were knocked silly.

Stanley looked around him at four unconscious killers. He looked up to heaven and said, "Thank you, dear Lloyd."

Then Stanley sprinted for freedom.

Stanley Stupid Strikes! 7

At the weapons arsenal on base, the colonel was supervising several of his soldiers who were loading weapons onto a transfer truck. A private with a clipboard watched the work, checking off items as they were loaded. He wasn't part of the colonel's plot, so he was wondering where all these weapons were going. He handed the clipboard to the colonel for his signature.

The colonel signed his name and handed back the clipboard. "There you go, Private."

The private said hesitantly, "Thank you, sir. And if you don't mind my asking, where exactly are you taking all this stuff on such short notice?"

The soldiers stopped loading. They all looked at the private and the colonel.

The colonel raised his eyebrows. "I'm sorry, soldier. Is there a new military chain of command that I'm unaware of? Is it now the business of a private to interrogate and harass a colonel?"

The private took a step back. He swallowed hard. "No sir . . ."

The colonel shouted, "Darn right it isn't! Now, drop and give me fifty!"

"Yes sir!" The private hit the ground and started doing push-ups.

The colonel smiled a little. He climbed into the transport truck. As the truck pulled away, he watched the private still doing push-ups. He shook his head. "I'm going to miss the army."

Back in the station wagon outside the main gate of the base, the Stupids were concluding their election. Buster counted the three ballots.

He looked up in a panic. "We've got a problem. The polls are *dead* even, give or take a vote."

Petunia's brow furrowed. "If only we knew who Dad was voting for!"

Suddenly Stanley appeared. He ran toward them, waving his arms. "Joan! Joan!"

Petunia stuck out her hand to her mom. "Congratulations, Mom." She figured her father's shouting was as good as a vote.

Joan was a good winner. "Thank you, everyone. As president, I appoint Stanley Stupid head of the army."

Stanley fell against the car, gasping for breath.

Joan pointed at her huffing husband. "Your first duty is to go into that army base and rescue my husband."

Buster added, "And get our dad while you're at it."

Stanley held up his hands. "I'm afraid those two will just have to wait. We've got to get to a place called Warehouse Twenty-one!"

He reached through the car window and took the keys from Joan. Then he ran around the car and jumped into the passenger's side. He put the key in the glove compartment lock.

He turned the key several times in the lock. He said tensely, "The car won't start!"

Petunia leaned forward and gave important instructions. "Dad, you and Mom switch places."

Stanley and Joan both leapt out of the car. They each ran around the front of the vehicle and got back in. Joan tried turning the key in the glove compartment too. When the car still didn't start, she and Stanley looked at the kids.

Buster said very carefully, "Mom, hand the keys to Dad."

Joan pulled the keys out of the glove compartment lock. She handed them to Stanley. He put them into the ignition. This time when he turned the keys, the car started.

Stanley shouted happily, "Good work, everyone!"

Shortly the Stupids' car was racing down the road. Joan asked, "Stanley?"

"Yes, Joan?"

"Where exactly is Warehouse Twenty-one, anyway?"

Stanley shrugged. "I don't know. But when the time comes, I trust the Lloyd will give us a sign."

Just then they saw a road sign that read WAREHOUSE 21. There was an arrow pointing up a side street.

Stanley smiled. "It's called having faith, Joan."

He drove into the abandoned warehouse district. It was a dark, dank, dirty, and deserted part of town. He parked the car on a grimy street.

Stanley stepped out of the car. "This must be the place."

Nearby, they saw the gray bulk of Warehouse 21. The sound of machinery grinding from inside the warehouse cut through the dismal silence of the area.

Stanley gathered his family around him for a pep talk. "It's not going to be a picnic in there. True, some people may have sandwiches. You may see the occasional side of potato salad. But don't be fooled. It's not a picnic. I simply can't stress that enough."

Buster said, "You're coming in loud and clear, Dad."

Stanley said, "Then let's do it."

The Stupids started down the dark street toward Warehouse 21. They moved in single file, creeping along, keeping an eye out for problems.

They didn't see two armed guards hiding behind a bush near the warehouse. But the guards saw the Stupids. One guard raised his rifle, but the other pushed it back down. The second guard put his finger to his lips. They were supposed to be quiet. Then the second guard brought out a crossbow and several arrows that were as long as his arm.

He loaded the crossbow. Then he aimed at the oncoming Stupids. He fired, but the arrow went wide. It zipped past the Stupids and hit an old wooden telephone pole. The Stupids didn't see the arrow.

Buster was last in line. He noticed the long arrow sticking out of the telephone pole as he went by.

He raised a curious eyebrow. "And what have we here?"

Buster reached out and grabbed the shaft of the arrow. He yanked on it, trying to pull it out of the pole. The arrow didn't budge. But the pole did. The telephone pole tilted as Buster kept pulling on the arrow. Finally the pole tipped over and crashed down to the ground. The telephone pole smashed— *wham!*—right into the bush where the two guards were hiding.

Petunia turned around to Buster. "Shhh!"

Buster whispered to her, "Sorry."

He kicked some dirt into the hole where the pole had been standing. Then he rushed to catch up with the rest of his family. They all began to climb a metal staircase that led up the outside of the warehouse.

Not far away, the Reverend Wright's limousine was parked outside a run-down house. There was a sign on the house that read THE REVEREND WRIGHT'S HALF-

WAY HOUSE. It was a place where ex-convicts lived. All the men in the house were tough former criminals. When they left prison, they had nowhere to go. So they came here. And they were loyal to the reverend, who they thought was a man of God.

Inside, one ex-con said to the reverend, "It means so much to have you visit the halfway house, Reverend Wright. In prison, you were the guiding light that beamed down upon so many of us."

The reverend smiled and looked humble. "I am thankful, my children, for the opportunities I've had to help you. And now, perhaps some of you can help me." He looked sad. "You see, there's someone out there who wants to harm your friend the reverend . . ."

Across the room, the assistant was talking to several other former convicts. "And then he looked at me with guileless eyes and said . . ." The assistant repeated Stanley's words. "Have faith, my son. For a man will come to repair all that is broken." He placed his hand over his heart. "And I know he was talking about my sinful soul."

Another of the ex-cons asked, "But Wright says this man's an enemy of the ministry. Are you telling us to question the reverend?"

The assistant clutched a briefcase tightly. He looked at it, then at the ex-con. The assistant looked very guilty. "There is much about the reverend you don't know."

Yet another ex-convict rushed into the room. He

ran up to the Reverend Wright. "Sir, one of our flock has spotted the car you were looking for in the warehouse district."

The Reverend Wright nodded solemnly. "Come. It is time to meet the man of whom I speak."

The assistant whispered to the convicts around him, "And when you meet him, you will understand."

Back at Warehouse 21, the Stupids slipped through a door near the top of the building. They found themselves standing on a metal catwalk high above the floor of the warehouse. They all looked down.

The warehouse was huge. It was like a giant airplane hangar. In the middle of the floor was the colonel's military transport truck loaded with weapons. There were boxes and crates stacked all over the place. They were labeled HIGH EXPLOSIVES.

The warehouse was crowded, with more than fifty people moving in all directions. The international military men, terrorists, and thugs unloaded all sorts of arms and weapons from the truck. They carried them back to their own trucks and Jeeps and cars. One soldier was huge. He was strong enough to lift large, heavy crates that would normally take two men to carry.

It was a dangerous situation. Some of the most vicious men in the world were in Warehouse 21. Anyone who would try to take them on would have to be a fool. Or a Stupid.

Stanley leaned over the railing of the scaffolding where his family stood. He shouted down. His voice echoed in the large warehouse.

"Excuse me, everyone," he called out. "May I have your attention, please?"

At the sound of Stanley's voice, the colonel and the lieutenant looked up into the dimness high over their heads. They saw Stanley and exchanged glances of disbelief.

The colonel breathed, "Impossible."

The lieutenant said, "He's amazing."

Stanley shouted, "Before you unleash strife and warfare upon this planet, look into your hearts. . . ."

Several soldiers raised their weapons. They all aimed at Stanley. The colonel raised his hand to stop them.

The colonel growled, "No guns!" He pointed to all the crates of explosives surrounding them.

Stanley continued his speech. "Inside, you're still human beings! You can change your ways. It's not too late to come back from the dark side . . ."

The colonel moved among the dangerous terrorists and soldiers. He snapped orders. "You—send a squad of men toward the eastern flank of the warehouse." He pointed at another group. "You—organize a counter to the right." Then to a third, "Your troops will back the first two squads, while my men rove on point."

One of the international terrorists looked puzzled. He pointed up at Stanley. "But he's only one man."

The colonel gazed up at Stanley with a look of fierce hatred. "Trust me. You don't want to underestimate him."

Up on the catwalk, Stanley was finishing his speech. "So turn yourselves in, everyone. My family and I do not want to fight you. But unless you give up, you'll leave us no choice."

From the shadows, Petunia asked her father, "Are they giving up?"

Stanley shaded his eyes and peered down into the distant floor of the warehouse. "No. In fact, they seem to be organizing some kind of massive attack."

Stanley sighed. He took off his coat and adjusted his suspenders. "I guess they want to do this the hard way."

Buster said, "They seem pretty well armed, Dad."

Stanley turned to his son. "Yes, Buster, but so are we. Oh, they may have guns and knives and bombs and missiles. But we're armed with the fact that we're doing what's right. And sometimes you just have to trust in that."

He turned and raced for the edge of the catwalk. He leapt up and sailed over the railing headfirst. Even though he was falling many, many feet, he wasn't worried.

For a brief second, the arms dealers all gazed skyward at the unbelievable sight. Stanley Stupid descended on them like a big diving bird of justice.

Then Stanley's suspenders caught on a hook that was dangling from the ceiling. They stretched, lowering him down to the floor like a bungee jumper. He landed gently on his feet, right in front of the colonel. His suspenders were stretched as far as they could go.

Stanley went into a martial arts stance. "Let the final showdown begin."

Two soldiers grabbed Stanley by the arms. His taut suspenders snapped back, lifting Stanley off the ground. The soldiers were flung high into the air in two directions.

Another soldier drew a bead on the rising Stanley with his rifle.

"Don't shoot!" the colonel ordered.

But it was too late. The soldier had already fired—*bang!* The bullet missed the fast-moving Stanley. It hit the warehouse ceiling and began to ricochet around the vast building.

All the bad guys froze in position. They followed the *ping! ping! ping!* as the bullet bounced from wall to floor to wall to ceiling again. It finally hit a box of explosives and it went off *ba whoom!* Wood and dust and dirt and metal flew around the warehouse.

Stanley was near the ceiling, so he wasn't hurt by the explosion. But as he was coming back down, the hook that held his suspenders broke. Stanley plummeted the last few feet into the center of a vast maze created by all the crates and boxes.

The colonel dusted himself off. He shouted, "Get him!"

Squads of soldiers rushed into the maze of crates, searching for Stanley.

Two police officers sat in their squad car several blocks from the warehouse. They heard the sound of a distant explosion.

One cop said, "What was that?"

His partner said, "Sounds to me like it came from the warehouse district."

They looked at each other and nodded. The driver stepped on the gas and they raced toward Warehouse 21.

Lines of soldiers were hunting Stanley through the crates. The stacks of boxes were ten feet high or more. No one could see over them. The soldiers marched in single file through the narrow paths running between the crates.

Stanley scurried through the paths. He was trying to stay ahead of the soldiers. From the catwalk high above, the other Stupids shouted down instructions. They could see the soldiers and Stanley. They yelled, "Left! Left! Right! Left!" He turned every corner in the direction they shouted as they led him away from the soldiers.

But then Stanley made a wrong turn. He came face-to-face with a group of soldiers.

The troops lifted the rifles waist high. Their guns had long, deadly bayonets. The soldiers began to advance.

Stanley backed up.

The squad leader told his troops, "Take your time, men. He's unarmed."

Stanley said, "Or *am* I?"

He looked around. He spotted an exposed water pipe running along the wall behind him. He quickly reached up and unscrewed a section of the pipe.

Stanley lifted the pipe over his head. "Ah-hah!" He was amazed at how resourceful he could be under pressure.

The squad of armed killers chuckled at him. They weren't scared of one man holding a metal pipe. They were a group of highly trained fighters with rifles and bayonets. They started to move toward Stanley again. They intended to finish him off.

Suddenly a deep, rumbling sound was heard from inside the wall. A powerful rush of water blasted out of the pipe that Stanley had unscrewed. The water hit the soldiers with the force of a cannon. They were driven back into a tall stack of crates. When the troops hit the boxes, the heavy stack collapsed on top of them.

The other three Stupids applauded wildly from the catwalk high above.

Petunia was smiling. "I'm getting a certain voyeuristic pleasure out of this."

Buster asked, "What's *voyeuristic* mean?"

Petunia screwed up her face and put her hands on her hips. "You're asking me? I'm like nine years old."

* * *

The Reverend Wright's limousine was speeding through the night toward the warehouse district. Wright was thinking about how he was going to get rid of Stanley. He could think of a lot of ways to do it.

The assistant sat in the backseat with several ex-convicts. He was quietly telling them more about Stanley. "And that's when he directed me to Peter 6:25. *Repent before the hour of judgment comes.*"

The ex-cons all nodded in agreement and murmured among themselves.

Television Can Save Your Life

Stanley screwed the water pipe back into place. He dusted his hands, satisfied. Then he turned around and saw the giant soldier facing him—the guy who had carried incredibly heavy boxes all by himself. The soldier grinned goofily. Then he reached over and picked up a crate that weighed at least five hundred pounds. He staggered, but he still moved toward Stanley.

Stanley looked around frantically for a way out. "I'm caught. I'm stuck. I'm trapped. Somebody help me out here!"

Petunia yelled a suggestion. "I'm cornered!"

"Yes!" Stanley shouted. "That's the word I was looking for. I'm cornered!"

Buster called out, "I'll save you, Dad!"

Buster hopped over the railing of the catwalk to a

high stack of crates. He scrambled down the crates, which were sitting on a forklift. Buster climbed over the forklift. He didn't realize that he had stepped onto the LIFT lever. As Buster reached the floor, the forklift began to raise the stack of boxes.

Buster got a grip on the stack of crates. He had to find some way to beat the huge soldier who was threatening his dad. "Must concentrate . . ." He strained to lift the boxes. Amazingly, they actually started to rise off the ground. He didn't know that it was the forklift doing the lifting. Buster said in a strained voice, "Focus the power of mind over matter . . ." The boxes rose up over his head. "Channel every ounce of willpower . . ."

The monster man stomped toward Stanley.

Buster's crate was several feet off the ground. He shouted, "It's working. I've done it! Behold the superhuman power of Buster!"

But soon the crate rose higher than Buster. He held on to the box and it lifted him off the ground.

"Huh?" Buster looked at his feet, which were now dangling in the air. Now he was hanging on to the bottom of a wooden slat in the crate.

The huge soldier prepared to crush Stanley beneath the heavy crate.

Suddenly the wooden slat that Buster was dangling from cracked wide open. Thousands of bullets spilled out of the crate in a huge *whoosh!* A stream of bullets poured along the floor like a metal river.

The monster man lost his footing on the bullets.

He began to slip and slide. The crate tilted this way and that. He lost his balance and his feet flailed in all directions. He skated awkwardly away from Stanley. Then he fell over backward—*whump!* The crate the giant man was holding slammed onto the floor and exploded. The force of the blast brought down an entire wall of crates on top of him.

The police car skidded to a halt in front of Warehouse 21 just as the explosion went off. The second cop grabbed the radio.

"Car Fifteen requests backup in the warehouse district. Send squad cars immediately to Warehouse Twenty-one!"

Back at the *Daily Times* office, one reporter was typing on his computer. The second reporter raced up with a radio scanner.

He pointed to the radio, which was squawking loudly with lots of police calls. He asked, "Have you tuned into a police scanner lately? Something seriously weird's going on in the warehouse district."

The first reporter said, "You want to take a drive?"

The second reporter answered quickly. "I'll get my coat."

They rushed out of the *Daily Times* building.

Warehouse 21 was erupting in chaos. Everyone was shouting and yelling. They were searching for Stanley among the crates. Smoke filled the air. Jumbled piles of collapsed boxes lay everywhere.

Joan was concerned about her husband and son. She leaned over the railing of the catwalk and shouted down, "Buster, Stanley! Please be careful down there. There are little fires burning all over the place now."

Joan noticed a fire extinguisher hanging on the wall. When she reached for it, she saw another, bigger fire extinguisher farther down on the wall. She moved down a stairway and grabbed it. Then on the floor she saw an even better fire extinguisher. She went down and got it. She didn't know that this wasn't a fire extinguisher. It was a flamethrower.

She aimed the "fire extinguisher" at a nearby flame. She fired a long jet of flame along the ground. The asphalt floor of the warehouse was liquefied by the heat.

She looked at the flamethrower curiously. "This is the worst fire extinguisher I've ever seen."

Another squad of soldiers spotted Buster. He assumed a fighting stance and they charged him.

"I'm warning you—*stay back!*" Buster yelled.

The soldiers hit the stretch of floor that had been melted by Joan's flamethrower. All of them were suddenly stuck fast. Their feet were glued to the ground.

Buster raised his eyebrows and smirked at them. "Mind over matter."

The lieutenant was listening to a walkie-talkie. He could overhear police calls coming in. He heard a squad car calling in, "Car Fifteen, we are on our way!" He could also hear sirens in the background.

He yelled to the colonel. "The police are coming, sir. We've got to get out of here!"

The colonel was calm. "Don't worry. The police are on our side." He pulled a jacket out of his Jeep and tossed it to the lieutenant. The back of the jacket read U.S. MARSHAL. "As far as they know."

The lieutenant and the colonel both put on the jackets.

Then the lieutenant caught sight of Stanley trying to get through the chaos. He was still coming after them.

The lieutenant pointed to Stanley. "What about him, sir?"

The colonel ripped the canvas cover off the eighty-millimeter M224 Smart Bomb missile launcher with computer visual targeting system. "There's enough throw-weight here to wipe out an entire tank battalion." He aimed the viewfinder. Then he locked it on Stanley. "Hopefully it'll stop this guy."

The missile launcher's computer digitized Stanley's face. It fed the image into its memory bank. It confirmed the LOCK ON—TARGET command. The launch countdown began at ten minutes.

Police cars roared up outside Warehouse 21. Police officers leapt out of the cruisers. Terrorists and arms dealers were streaming from the warehouse. They began exchanging gunfire with the cops.

The colonel and the lieutenant slipped out of the warehouse. They were disguised as U.S. marshals. They blended in with the police officers.

The colonel called out to some nearby cops. "Shoot to kill, boys. Those are evil men in there."

The colonel and the lieutenant got into a car and drove away from the scene.

Behind the warehouse, the Reverend Wright's big white limousine skidded to a stop right behind the Stupids' station wagon.

The driver pointed to the car. "That's his car, sir."

The Reverend Wright said, "It's just a matter of time now."

The reverend and the ex-cons piled out of the limo.

A few seconds later, the two reporters drove up to the rear of the warehouse. One of them asked, "What is going on here?"

The second reporter yelled, "Hey, look! That's Reverend Wright's limo over there."

"Pull over!" the first reporter shouted.

They parked behind the reverend's limousine.

Nearby, the Natural History Museum van was stopped by a police officer. Charles Sender was driving the van. The cop leaned in.

"I'm sorry, sir," the police officer said, "but no one's getting through at the moment."

Sender looked a little upset. "Oh dear." He looked at his watch. "I suppose I'd better find another route home." He pulled a city map out of the glove compartment.

The police officer said, "In the meantime, please pull your vehicle over with the rest of them."

The cop pointed to a row of cars—the Stupids' station wagon, the Reverend Wright's limousine, and the reporters' car.

Back inside the warehouse, the Stupids reunited.

Joan said proudly, "Oh, Stanley, you were so brave out there! Are you all right?"

Stanley said, "I'm fine, Joan."

Suddenly his pants dropped to his ankles!

Stanley grabbed his pants and pulled them up. "My suspenders, however, were lost in the battle."

The Stupids moved to an exit at the back of the warehouse. They walked past the missile launcher. They noticed the countdown clock ticking.

Stanley said, "Hey! It looks to me as if this missile is set to launch in five minutes."

Petunia agreed. "It looks that way to me too."

"Me too," Buster said.

"Me too," Joan chimed in.

Stanley did some quick calculations and said, "So among the four of us, we've got just twenty minutes to get out of here. Let's go!"

The Reverend Wright was standing outside the back door of the warehouse. He was glaring evilly at the door, waiting for Stanley to emerge. The assistant looked even more nervous and troubled.

The reverend growled, "Here he comes. The moment of reckoning has arrived."

The assistant moaned, "The moment of reckoning indeed."

Just as the Stupids came out the door, there was a tremendous explosion deep in the warehouse behind them. Stanley stepped out through a billowing cloud of white smoke.

The ex-cons were impressed by this magnificent spectacle. They all went, "Ooooh . . ."

Stanley looked at them. But behind them he saw Sender sitting beside the road, studying his map.

"Sender!" Stanley yelled.

The Reverend Wright looked confused. "What did he say?"

"He said, 'Sinner,' " the assistant screamed. "And he's talking about me!"

Wright stared angrily at his assistant. "Not now, you idiot. Get ahold of yourself."

The assistant broke down. "No, I can't pretend anymore! I'm a wretched man! I've helped you skim money from your followers, cheat on your taxes, defraud innocent people!"

Wright tried to cover up. "Have you lost your mind? What are you talking about?"

The assistant held up the briefcase that he always carried. "It's all in here!"

The two reporters stepped up behind him. One said, "We're from the *Daily Times*. Mind if we look at that?"

The Reverend Wright turned to the ex-convicts. "Stop him! Destroy them! What are you waiting for? Do what I say!"

The ex-cons were unsure what to do.

The Stupids passed by the reverend. Stanley said to him, "Looks like you got here a little late. The battle's mostly over now."

Wright shook his fist at Stanley. "Over? You turn my followers against me, tear down my empire, and try to tell me it's over? I'm Reverend Wright!" He pulled out a pistol and aimed at Stanley. "And this isn't over until I've made you pay!"

Suddenly two police officers rushed in and tackled Wright. They grabbed the gun away from him.

The ex-cons all turned to look in awe at Stanley. One of them said, "The prophecies of the newcomer have come true."

Another convict said, "He has opened our eyes."

A third ex-con proclaimed, "He shall be our new leader."

The first ex-con called out, "We must strive to be more like him."

Just then Stanley's pants fell down again. All of the ex-cons started to drop their pants in reverent imitation. Stanley lifted his pants.

He said to his family, "Well, our work here is done. But before we go, there's a certain archvillain I'd like to talk to. I've got a feeling he learned a pretty important lesson today."

Stanley passed the three ex-cons, with their pants

around their ankles, and walked up to Sender. The museum director was still looking at the road map.

Stanley said, "Well, my friend. It seems you lost."

Sender turned the map around in his hands. "I certainly am."

Stanley advised him. "The problem is, you went down the wrong road right from the start."

Sender looked up at Stanley. "Can you help me get back on the path?"

"Yes, I can, but it won't be easy. You've got to turn yourself around. You've got to straighten out. But as long as you remember to head toward the light, you can't go wrong."

Sender stood up and shook Stanley's hand. "Thanks. You've really saved me."

Stanley smiled. "Until we meet again."

Sender got back in his van and drove away.

Buster stood next to Stanley. "I can't believe it, Dad. First you defeat the army of the underworld, then you reform the greatest criminal of our time."

Stanley put his arm around his son's shoulder. "It just goes to show you, Buster. Good things happen to good people."

Inside the warehouse, the missile launcher countdown reached zero. The missile blasted off and zoomed out of the building. It screeched straight for Stanley. And Stanley didn't realize it.

Stanley's pants fell down. He bent over to grab them, and the missile *whooshed* over him. It roared up into the air and banked around to come at him again.

One of the ex-cons saw it and shouted, "Reverend Stupid, look out!"

Stanley looked up and saw the missile coming his way. He jumped into his station wagon and floored the gas pedal. The car roared off down the street with the missile in pursuit.

The missile's visual computer lost track of Stanley as he wheeled the car onto the highway. The missile moved higher into the sky to look for him. It was a really smart Smart Bomb, and, after a while, the sophisticated equipment locked onto the airport. It dived down and saw Stanley's car. It was parked and Stanley was not in it.

The missile zipped past the car. Using the on-board video camera, it followed Stanley's likely path. The missile flew through the airline ticket office. Then it passed through the boarding gate. It cruised out over the runway, where a jetliner was just taking off.

It saw Stanley through one of the jets!

Stanley looked out the window of the plane and saw the approaching missile. He raced up the aisle and into the cockpit.

The pilot and copilot turned and looked at him in surprise.

Stanley said, "No time to explain!" He tore open a storage locker and pulled out a parachute. He strapped it on. Then he kicked open an emergency door and jumped out.

As he skydived, the missile charged him several

times. Stanley curled up into a ball. The missile roared past—*whoosh!* He twisted his waist. *Swish!* He spread his legs. *Fwaash!*

He looked down at the city below him. The ground was coming up very fast. He pulled the rip cord on the parachute. The chute popped open and Stanley slowly drifted to the earth.

Now he was a sitting duck. The missile turned for one final attack. Stanley couldn't dodge anymore. He closed his eyes and waited for the end.

Meanwhile, the colonel and the lieutenant walked down a quiet city street below him. The colonel stuffed the U.S. marshal's jacket into a trash can.

The lieutenant said, "I can't believe it, sir. We made it!"

The colonel shrugged. "It's like I've been telling you, Lieutenant. Good things happen to bad people." He lit up a cigar. "Anyone who thinks otherwise is just plain stupid."

They strolled past the window of a department store. The window was full of televisions. And on every single television was Stanley's face. The announcer was saying, "Then at eleven, it's an encore presentation of *Debbie*, where you'll meet a man who claims to be his own grandpa . . ."

Suddenly, high above, the missile screeched to an abrupt stop in midair. It turned ninety degrees and went into a power dive straight down.

Stanley slowly opened his eyes and watched the

missile streak away from him. He couldn't figure it out.

The missile's Smart Bomb tracking computer locked onto the department store window full of Stanley Stupid faces. It screamed down at supersonic speed, arming its warhead for maximum destruction.

The colonel and the lieutenant both looked up at the sound of the missile's rocket engines. Then they looked at each other. The missile hit and there was a massive explosion.

The next day, Stanley was standing at the barbecue grill in his backyard. He wore a chef's hat and an apron.

His neighbor stepped out to get the newspaper. He waved at Stanley and called out, "Haven't seen you around much this weekend, Stanley. What've you been up to?"

Stanley shrugged. "Oh, this and that. Had breakfast. Read the paper. Saved the world."

The neighbor cocked one eyebrow at Stanley. "Is that right?"

"Yes, you know my family. When we get together, anything can happen. Say, today I thought we'd relax and have a barbecue. Why not stop by?" Stanley opened up a package of ground beef and began cutting it with a weed whacker. "There's plenty for everyone!"

At the Stupids' picnic table, Joan stuck the hose of a bicycle pump into a watermelon. Petunia started pumping. *Boom!* The watermelon exploded into little pieces.

Buster grabbed a piece of watermelon and went to the grill. "This is going to be great, Dad! Say, how can I help?"

Stanley said, "Well, you can flip the burgers, son. But you'd better let me handle the lighter fluid. See this?"

Stanley turned the can of lighter fluid upside down and showed Buster the warning label on the bottom. KEEP . . . OUT . . . OF REACH . . . OF CHILDREN.

As he read the label, the lighter fluid drained from the can. It made a trail that ran down the driveway and over to a truck carrying propane gas that was parked across the street. Stanley pulled out a match to light the charcoals. He tossed the match over his shoulder, and it landed in the trail of lighter fluid. The flame *whooshed* up and ran quickly down the driveway and into the street.

Before it reached the truck, the fire was put out by a stream of water from a hose. The dog stood at the end of the driveway with the garden hose. The cat worked the spigot with her little paws.

Then both pets looked at the Stupids. The family was having a good time at their backyard barbecue and hadn't noticed a thing. The dog rolled his eyes. The cat looked at the dog and shook her head. Then they both smiled.